Drew made her th___ she had no business thinking and feeling, because the places they led were dangerous.

He leaned in a little closer, resting his arm along the back of her chair. He was so close, she could feel the heat of his body and smell the intoxicating scent of him. It made her want to breathe in a little deeper.

Drew left her breathless—or maybe it was just the physical reaction of a woman wanting a man who seemed to want her back. Why make it any more complicated than it was?

Sometimes a girl just had to say what the hell and go for broke with the gorgeous guy who'd been flirting with her since the moment they'd first laid eyes on each other.

Even if it wasn't going to last longer than the moment…or the night.

Dear Reader,

As a romance writer, I feel very blessed to be living my dream. I sometimes work long hours and when I'm on deadline my social life seems nonexistent, but other than being a wife and mother I can't think of anything I'd rather do with my life. In the world of romance, my heart is at home. I wish this same sense of belonging to everyone.

So does Drew Montogmery, my hero in *Texas Magic*. Drew is a newspaperman with an unshakable conviction that people aren't really living unless they go after what they want in life. If not, then what's the point? This notion is an epiphany for heroine Caroline Coopersmith. Even though Caroline seems to have it all, she is living the life that her father has sculpted for her as his heir apparent. It's not what Caroline wants, but she feels beholden to family tradition. It's only when Drew makes her realize that she has spent way too many years doing what's expected of her, not what she wants, that she is able to fall in love and live her dream.

I hope you'll enjoy Drew and Caroline's story, which is book two in my Celebrations, Inc. series. Please be sure to look for the final book in this series, *Texas Christmas*, in November. And be sure to let me know what you think of them. You can reach me at nrobardsthompson@yahoo.com.

May all your dreams come true,

Nancy Robards Thompson

TEXAS MAGIC

NANCY ROBARDS THOMPSON

HARLEQUIN®

entertain, enrich, inspire™

This book is dedicated to Kathleen O'Brien
and Lori Harris.

Recycling programs
for this product may
not exist in your area.

ISBN-13: 978-0-373-65700-1

TEXAS MAGIC

Copyright © 2012 by Nancy Robards Thompson

www.Harlequin.com

Printed in U.S.A.

Books by Nancy Robards Thompson

Harlequin Special Edition

†*Fortune's Unexpected Groom* #2185
**Texas Wedding #2214
**Texas Magic #2218

Silhouette Special Edition

Accidental Princess #1931
Accidental Cinderella #2002
**The Family They Chose* #2026
Accidental Father #2055
Accidental Heiress #2082

Harlequin NEXT

Out with the Old, In with the New
What Happens in Paris (Stays in Paris?)
Sisters
True Confessions of the Stratford Park PTA
Like Mother, Like Daughter (But in a Good Way)
  "*Becoming My Mother…*"
Beauty Shop Tales
An Angel in Provence

*The Baby Chase
†The Fortunes of Texas: Whirlwind Romance
**Celebrations, Inc.

Other books by this author available in ebook format.

NANCY ROBARDS THOMPSON

Award-winning author Nancy Robards Thompson is a sister, wife and mother who has lived the majority of her life south of the Mason-Dixon line. As the oldest sibling, she reveled in her ability to make her brother laugh at inappropriate moments, and she soon learned she could get away with it by proclaiming "What? I wasn't doing anything." It's no wonder that upon graduating from college with a degree in journalism, she discovered that reporting "just the facts" bored her silly. Since she hung up her press pass to write novels full-time, critics have deemed her books "funny, smart and observant." She loves chocolate, champagne, cats and art (though not necessarily in that order). When she's not writing, she enjoys spending time with her family, reading, hiking and doing yoga.

Chapter One

Dark chocolate for a white wedding.

The juxtaposition brought a smile to Maya LeBlanc's lips as she stood at the worktable in the kitchen of Maya's Chocolaterie, threading the last sterling-silver heart charm onto the final strand of white satin ribbon. Savoring the scent of roasted cocoa beans, cinnamon and dried rose petals that lingered in the air, she tied a bow on the last box of wedding favors and placed it on the baker's rack with the other 349 she had already put together. Each small package contained a quartet of hand-made truffles—an exclusive recipe she had concocted specifically for the Coopersmith/Harris wedding, which would take place at the end of the week across the Atlantic Ocean in Celebration, Texas.

Nothing that came out of Maya's kitchen was mass-produced. In fact, all of the chocolates she made were as exclusive as the occasions and clients for whom she designed them.

However, she wasn't accustomed to producing her sweets on this large of a scale: fourteen hundred truffles in three days. The wedding chocolate—in addition to what she needed to sustain her shop's daily business—was a tall order that took more manpower than Maya, in her tiny St. Michel shop, possessed. She had put in a lot of extra hours this week after she had turned over the Shop Closed sign. Now that she was finished and staring at the mountainous pile of white boxes, she wasn't sure she would ever take on another task of such epic proportions. But she blinked away the thought, feeling like a first-time marathon runner who had just crossed the finish line and was already contemplating her next race.

Maya had done this order as a favor for her friend Caroline Coopersmith, the sister of the bride. Despite the fact that Maya had never met Caroline's sister, Claudia, she couldn't say no after hearing the desperation in Caroline's voice. Apparently, Claudia was more aptly described as Bridezilla on the rampage than blushing bride to be. The Texas-based chocolatier originally procured to provide the truffles for Claudia's wedding had gone out of business, disappearing lock, stock and bridal favors into the night with Claudia's deposit—one week before the wedding.

While individual boxes of truffles for the guests would not make or break the wedding, Bridezilla was breathing fire and Caroline had called Maya, desperate for her to work her magic: produce an exclusive confection for the occasion and ship it to the States in a matter of days.

"It wouldn't hurt if you sent a special box made with ingredients that will calm my sister's nerves," Caroline had joked.

Hmmm...not a bad idea. Some chamomile and lavender in white chocolate. That was a good start, and Maya had been stewing on it as she finished up the large order.

She glanced at her watch. It was nearly two in the morning, which made it just before eight o'clock in the evening in Texas. She picked up the telephone and dialed Caroline's cell phone number.

Caroline picked up on the third ring. "Hello?"

"Bonjour! It's Maya." She settled into a chair, trying not to let the fatigue that suddenly weighed on her like an anchor show in her voice. "Fait accompli. Tell your sister to rest assured that the order will arrive in plenty of time for the wedding. I will package the truffles in foam coolers and ship them to you tomorrow. Tout de suite!"

"You're wonderful! And you must be a mind reader, because not ten minutes ago Claudia called asking for an update on the chocolate. I told her I'd call you tomorrow since it was late in St. Michel. I hope this job hasn't cost you too much sleep."

"Sleep is overrated. How are your sister's wedding plans progressing?"

As Caroline sighed, Maya sensed that her friend was even more exhausted than she was.

"At the risk of sounding like a terrible sister, I will be so glad when Saturday arrives and the wedding is over. The world will stop revolving around Claudia and we will all be able to reclaim our lives. I'm happy for her, really, I am. But just when I think she can't possibly drain one more ounce out of the bridal party, she manages to draw blood."

Caroline sighed again. "I'm sorry, Maya. I must sound like a miserable person."

A note in Caroline's Texan drawl made Maya

think that perhaps the weariness was the product of more than physical exhaustion. Hmmm… a box of something special for Caroline was in order, too.

"No, you don't sound like a *misérable* person. You're a fabulous sister for doing all that you have for her. Do you have a date for the wedding?" Ever the matchmaker, Maya couldn't resist asking.

"Are you kidding? Between work at the accounting firm, baking for the catering company and my maid-of-honor duties, I barely have time to sleep. There are no men on my horizon."

Ahh…that explained it. Being maid of honor in a wedding when you had no love of your own was like being trapped inside a candy store and not being allowed to taste the sweets. Seeing the possibilities and imagining what it might be like, but that's where it ended.

Alas, Caroline deserved more.

An idea swelled up inside of Maya, like a perfect chocolate soufflé rising in the oven.

Yes, it's Caroline's turn for love.

And Maya knew just the thing to set the wheels of love in motion.

Caroline Coopersmith helped herself to a large piece of wedding cake and carried it to the empty bridal-party table. All of the other attendants were on the dance floor. Here Caroline was, getting cozy with a plate of fat and sugar. She decided she might as well have another glass of champagne, too.

She waved over a waiter, grabbed a flute and then slipped her feet out of the four-inch stilettos that were so painful they should have carried a warning label. For the first time that evening— actually, for the first time in *months*—Caroline was able to inhale a full, deep breath and relax.

Her sister, Claudia, was married.

At long last.

The relief Caroline felt did not solely have to do with the fact that her aching feet had been mercifully freed from bondage. It was more to do with everyone making it through the wedding unscathed. No one had killed Claudia. Nor did the more plausible threat of Claudia killing or maiming *her* come to fruition.

Now, Caroline was free. And she had cake and champagne....

What more could a girl want?

Caroline's gaze searched the room for best man Drew Montgomery. Before she could find him, something else caught her eye.

Claudia waved from the center of the crowded

dance floor, motioning her to join in a group
dance to the Black Eyed Peas's "I Gotta Feeling."
Caroline's gaze swept the dance floor, searching.
When she still did not see Drew among the rev-
elers, any motivation she might have mustered
to drag herself into the fray evaporated. Living
up to his job description, Drew certainly was the
best man here. And probably the only thing more
tempting than the wedding cake.

She and Drew had met for the first time yesterday at the rehearsal. Since he was best man to
her maid of honor, the two had been paired up at
the rehearsal dinner last night. It had been nice
meeting him and spending time with him.

Caroline smiled but shook her head, raising
her glass to her sister in a "go ahead without me"
toast.

Claudia flashed a quick okay sign and turned
back to her groom, Kyle, who pulled her close,
folding her into their own private slow dance to
the fast song. They kissed and looked so in love,
as if they had not a care in the world.

And they didn't, really. Caroline sighed and ate
a bite of cake as she watched them. At least right
now they didn't have a care. The wedding had
gone off without a hitch. All that was left was the
bridal bouquet toss and the send-off. After that

her sister and new brother-in-law would ride off into their future, and Caroline would be free to retreat to her hotel suite and enjoy a long, hot soak in the pond-sized marble Jacuzzi tub.

In the meantime, she had carrot cake with cognac-spiked hazelnut marzipan crème filling. She closed her lips around another generous bite and closed her eyes, savoring the delectable combination of flavors.

Hazelnuts…cloves…nutmeg…

If she had made this wedding cake herself, she would've added a dash more cinnamon…and maybe a hint of orange zest to the filling—a secret *something* to lend a certain je ne sais quois.…

Baking was her hobby, the happy place she went to when she needed to ground herself. Given the stressful nature of her job with Coopersmith & Bales, the accounting firm her great-grandfather had founded, she found herself retreating more and more into the sweet goodness of her confectionary sanctuary. Because baking was the only thing that kept her sane. It was a wonder she did not weigh five hundred pounds.

Still, even without the flavors Caroline would add, the cake was heavenly. She opened her eyes to fork up another bite. On the dance floor, Kyle dipped Claudia and the guests cheered. The surprised delight on her sister's face made Caroline smile, too. Claudia looked so beautiful…and in love.

Yes, all was right with the world. How could it not be when there was a living, breathing example of true love right in front of her?

Watching the love between her sister and brother-in-law renewed her faith in true love, even though her own romantic future did not seem very bright. She had had plenty of boyfriends over the years but never a serious relationship.

Why? Because Caroline was so very guarded. It was one of her flaws, and she readily admitted it. Still, it also happened that most of the men she had dated—the ones who might have had the potential to work out—always seemed to be unavailable, preoccupied or headed somewhere: off to college or internships or jobs. Or some of them just weren't in a good place for a relationship. There always seemed to be an obstacle that stood in the way. Real or imagined, it was Caroline's justification for keeping up the walls of self-protection.

This weekend, though, she thought she had felt a spark of mutual attraction between Drew and herself, but he'd been scarce since the wedding party and family dances had ended.

That was fine. Disappointing, but, really, what had she expected?

Well, at one point, she had actually admitted to herself that if she were the type of woman who had one-night stands, Drew Montgomery was exactly the kind of guy she would choose. He was a classic—tall, dark and handsome, with broad shoulders and a hint of irreverent bad boy that added to his allure.

It was crazy that she had even considered something so out of character. But she was a grown woman—thirty-three years old, for God's sake. She had no prospects in sight and no time in her busy schedule to think about going out on a manhunt. And again, was it so wrong to want a taste of romance for herself…no matter how fleeting?

With all eyes on Claudia and Kyle this weekend, and delicious Drew at her side…well, it had been a tempting daydream.

Thank God, he was nowhere to be found in the dangerous hour when their wedding duties were done and the champagne was flowing like an endless river.

Wistful, Caroline turned her attention back to her plate, scraping up the last traces of icing. It was so good. She just might treat herself to seconds. There was nothing to feel guilty about, as long as she didn't consider the calories in the small box of Maya's truffles she had already consumed before the wedding had even started.

Along with the shipment of chocolate party favors, Maya had sent special boxes of truffles to Caroline and Claudia. She had called the treats "wedding survival kits." She had claimed that Claudia's chocolates contained calming herbs to help rid her of bridal jitters; observing how calm and carefree her sister seemed right now, they'd obviously worked their magic.

Caroline's box, Maya had said, was a reward for seeing Claudia through the wedding stress. Maya's note to Caroline had read: *Eat these on the day of the wedding, and remember, my sweet, a gracious maid of honor always gets her reward. L'amour!*

L'amour? Wouldn't that be a nice reward?

Again, her gaze scanned the dance floor for Drew. Coming up empty, she found herself back at square one, contemplating the crumbs on her clean cake plate. The only *l'amour* coming her way was another piece of cake.

She was in the process of sliding her feet back into her shoes—the price she had to pay for indulgence—when a deep voice startled her out of her reverie.

"This seat taken?"

Drew Montgomery did not wait for an answer. He was already folding himself into the chair next to Caroline. Of course, given the fact that the table was empty, his question was probably rhetorical.

Caroline checked her posture and felt the involuntary reflex of her fingers sweeping across her lips, checking for errant crumbs and stray smudges of icing. Now, as Drew sat next to her—and just where had he materialized from? Never mind that—now that he was here, the first piece of cake she had eaten felt like a rock in her gut. She inhaled slowly to settle her nerves, and the bodice of her dress felt tight. That second piece of cake…well, now it just seemed like a bad idea.

"I didn't get a chance to tell you this earlier, but nice dress." Drew's eyes, the same shade of dark brown as Maya's imported chocolates, sparkled with mischief. This was another side to the sexy man who tended to make her mouth go dry and her mind go blank when he walked into the room…especially now that he was sitting next to her. *Man,* he looked good in that tux.

Caroline forced herself to look out at the dance floor so she wouldn't stare at Drew. "Yeah, my sister promised us we'd get multiple uses out of it. What do you think? Is it suitable for a night on the town?"

She grabbed a fistful of pumpkin-colored taffeta and tulle underskirt and gave it a shake. It rustled like dry leaves in a trash bag.

As Drew took a long, slow draw of beer, his gaze meandered unselfconsciously from her handful of skirt, up the bodice of her dress, lingering a beat on her décolletage. She let go of the skirt and crossed her arms so that her forearm covered her cleavage and her hand rested at the base of her throat. His gaze resumed its journey, finally finding her eyes.

"Yeah, it's kind of noisy." Although he was nodding as if he approved. "But you wear it well, Caroline. Would be a shame to let it go to waste in the back of your closet. I say wear it and own it."

"Own the fact that I look like someone's Halloween pumpkin? I don't think so, Drew."

It wasn't just the way he held her gaze, it was the way his dark, curly hair fell across his forehead and the teasing tilt of his sideways grin that also did her in. Suddenly she wasn't quite so eager to retreat to that marble Jacuzzi tub…alone.

What if she asked him to join her?

Her cheeks burned at the thought.

He was her new brother-in-law's best friend.

Even though she had already dismissed the one-night-of-bliss fantasy, now that he was sitting here—so mesmerizingly close—she shouldn't be thinking of him in the getting-naked-in-a-Jacuzzi way, either. Because if she found herself naked in a Jacuzzi with him, then that would inevitably lead to the one-night stand, which she had already dismissed. She wasn't going to kid herself. With her workload at the firm and the extra hours she was putting in helping out her friend A. J. Sherwood-Antonelli baking desserts for Celebrations, Inc., a catering company, Caroline barely had time to sleep.

So, no, there was no time for a man in her life… well, beyond tonight, anyway. So maybe that was all the more reason she should put away her prude and just go for it.

She had to look away and bite the insides of her cheeks to rid herself of the thoughts that were ringing in her head right now. Not to mention, at this point she was surely the same shade of red as the cranberries in the table centerpieces.

What was wrong with her? Too much champagne? Sugar overload?

"Sugar," he said.

Great. And now he was reading her mind.

"Excuse me?"

"I was thinking you looked more like a sweet sugar pumpkin in that dress rather than a carving pumpkin." He grinned at her, relaxed and casual in his chair, obviously aware of how flustered he was making her. "There is a difference, you know? One of the reporters at the *Journal* just wrote an article about a pumpkin farm over in Celina. She said you should never use a big carving pumpkin for pie. It will be bitter. You have to use the small, firm sugar pumpkins. They're much sweeter."

Again, his eyes meandered the length of her dress.

Small, firm sugar pumpkins? Was he speaking metaphorically?

She shivered, but this time she did not cross her arms to hide herself. Instead, she blinked at him. "Is that supposed to be a compliment?"

"Yes, ma'am."

She reached out and swatted his arm. "If that's the best you can do, that's pathetic."

See, the other dangerous thing she had learned about Drew Montgomery this weekend was that he had a way of pulling her out of that awkward, tongue-tied mire she initially found herself in when she was with him, and then it was a slippery slope into the sea of longing. Tonight, it seemed, there was no life preserver to save her. No life-boat in which she could stash the bald truth: this man made her think and feel things she had no business thinking and feeling, because the places they led were dangerous.

He motioned to a woman carrying a tray of champagne. She wasted no time appearing at his side. Drew replaced Caroline's empty flute with a full one.

"Pathetic, huh?" he asked.

"Pretty much."

"Damn, I guess that means I'll have to make it up to you. Or at least prove to you that I'm not pathetic. At least not when it counts."

Good Lord, his smile was enough to push her over the edge of that slippery slope.

"Would you wear your sugar pumpkin dress out on the town if I wore this monkey suit? Tie and all—we match. See, pumpkin tie. Pumpkin dress." He motioned back and forth.

She blinked, unsure of what to say. If she let herself go there, she might believe he was asking her out on a date.

"But that would mean you'd have to rent the monkey suit again, and I'd have to postpone burning this hideous dress." She shook her head, feeling pretty clever for keeping up her end of the push-and-pull banter. "So, I don't think it will work."

He frowned and, oh, how she wanted to believe he really was disappointed by her pretend rebuff. This was simply casual flirting, but somehow it didn't feel like the brand of casual they'd established this weekend.

"Well, then, if you're turning me down for a date," he said, "the least you can do is make it up to me some other way."

Date? So he *was* asking her out on a real date? She in her hideous pumpkin-colored bridesmaid dress and he in his matching bow tie. That was a vision. Something in the mischievous look on his face hinted that he never took life seriously. She wasn't quite sure if he was serious about this pumpkin-themed date.

Still, play along…

"What exactly did you have in mind?" she asked.

"Right at this moment?" He smiled, grabbed another glass of champagne off a passing waiter's tray and set it in front of her.

She narrowed her eyes at him. "I'm onto your plans for the moment. You're trying to get me drunk. So, does that mean you plan on taking advantage of me?"

"Is that an option?" he asked. "Because if it's not, you're perfectly welcome to take advantage of *me*."

The dance beat slowed to something soulful and their gazes locked. The air between them shifted.

"You have to admit, Caroline, there's some serious chemistry between you and me. And I don't think you're going to be in any shape to catch the bride's bouquet until we do a couple of chemistry experiments and contain all this...you know—" he motioned back and forth between the two of them again "—this *energy*. Otherwise, it might throw you off your flower-catching game."

See? He'd done it again. He'd started off talking about the chemistry between them—a chemistry that was so real it was almost palpable. No one with eyes could deny that. But then he switched tracks to something light and funny, leaving the serious edge hanging between them. Still, Caroline was no dummy; she knew that when he defaulted to light and funny it was because what was happening between them was simply casual flirting.

So keep it casual, Caroline. Don't make this more difficult than it needs to be.

"Whoa there, Romeo, what makes you think I

want to catch the bridal bouquet? And don't you dare say all women want to catch the flowers."

"You don't like flowers?"

"I *love* flowers."

He leaned in a little closer, resting his arm along the back of her chair. He was so close, she could feel the heat of his body and smell the intoxicating scent of him. It made her want to breathe in a little deeper. Suddenly, she forgot her entire case against catching the bride's flowers. But then again she wasn't really going to make a case. She was keeping this light and casual.

"Then why wouldn't you want to catch them?" He whispered the words in her ear. His breath was hot on her cheek. It was all she could do to keep from dragging him straight up to that big marble Jacuzzi and having her way with him.

Instead, she reached out and ran her finger along the edge of his bow tie. Good lord, the man looked devastating in a tux, despite the dreadful pumpkin tie. Actually, it didn't look bad with his dark eyes and hair…and he was so close. All she would have to do was lean in a fraction of an inch and her lips would be touching his. The realization made her bite down on her lower lip.

"My philosophy," he said, "is you have to go

after what you want in life. If not, what's the point of living?"

His words hit home and were a little sobering. Why not go for something *she* wanted? Why not just this once do something completely out of character and take something just for herself? Even if it was impermanent…even if she could only have Drew for one night…

She had never slept with a guy before they were solidly in a committed relationship. The thought of getting physical with Drew left her breathless—or maybe it was the way Drew was looking at her. Whatever it was, something was different tonight. Was it the wedding? The champagne? Or maybe it was just the physical reaction of a woman wanting a man who seemed to want her back. Why make it any more complicated than it was?

His words echoed in her head, in her heart. *You have to go after what you want in life. If not, what's the point of living?*

She really had not been living, had she?

"There's definitely chemistry between us, Drew. But rather than trying to figure it all out, like a science experiment, don't you just want to enjoy the magic? You know, get lost in the fantasy? Science steals the magic because it explains too much. I happen to like fantasy even more than I like flowers."

"Science never was my thing," he said. "Maybe we should…dance, instead."

Chapter Two

Sometimes a girl just had to say *what the hell* and go for broke with the gorgeous guy who'd been flirting with her since the moment they'd first laid eyes on each other.

Even if it wasn't going to last longer than the moment...or the night.

Liquid courage wasn't fully to blame for Caroline turning a moment with Drew into a night. Nope, blame wasn't even a factor in this equation.

Although she would like to know what had come over her last night. She raised her chin as she peered at herself in the bathroom mirror, wiping away the remnants of stubborn makeup smudges that had not washed away in the shower.

They'd danced until the moment Claudia had tossed her bouquet. Claudia had looked Caroline in the eye, turned around and tossed the flowers right to her. There had been no running or lunging or fighting. With one clean toss, the bouquet had tumbled through the air in a surreal sort of slow motion, before it landed right in Caroline's hands.

Then, her sister and Kyle had gotten into the limo and had driven off into the night.

Caroline and Drew had wasted no time finding their way up to Caroline's hotel suite.

Yes, she had been perfectly in control of her choices. Even if nearly every move she had made since abandoning her second trip to the cake table had been out of character.

It was too late to second-guess herself. It was six o'clock in the morning and Drew had been sound asleep when she had tiptoed off to the shower. She took her time, thinking that if he awoke and wanted an easy out, he could dress and slip out while she was occupied in the other room.

No awkward morning-after dances…especially since their "dance" last night had been so perfect. She wanted the end of their tryst—God, was that what this was, a tryst? When was the last time she had used that word? Probably never. That's why she wanted the end of whatever this was to be as easy and unforced as the beginning: They'd danced during the reception after the limo had taken Claudia and Kyle away, Caroline and Drew had ended up back in her suite with a bottle of champagne, sharing the big marble Jacuzzi. Then they'd heated up the sheets of the big bed she initially thought would swallow her up alone.

But it had not. It had proven to be quite a lovely playground, where she and Drew Montgomery had played games she never dreamed she would take part in with someone like him.

He of all people. Her brother-in-law's best friend. Good Lord, if Claudia ever found out, her holier-than-thou sister would...well, she definitely wouldn't approve. As if Caroline's wedding "nightcap" might somehow sully Claudia's fairy-tale-perfect nuptials.

Caroline inhaled sharply, refusing to feel guilty over taking a little slice of pleasure for herself for a change. The scent of the lavender bath salts they'd used in the tub last night still perfumed the air.

Never in her life had Caroline felt so drawn to someone she knew so little about. The undeniable vibe she was getting from Drew this weekend was that he was the consummate bad boy. With his charm, she imagined he was a virtuoso at wooing women. The thought sent a particular thrill coursing through her.

Maybe she was overromanticizing the situation, but if she had learned one thing about Drew Montgomery this weekend it was that he had an unshakeable conviction to live life to its fullest.

If not, what's the point of living?

His words haunted her. Their influence had been the tipping point, and the rest was history. Granted, a very short chapter in Caroline's romantic history. But still, it was something.

Maybe he was onto something with his "authentic living" philosophy. Maybe she should borrow a page from that philosophy and tell her father that the stuffy offices of Coopersmith & Bales weren't where she wanted to spend the rest of her life.

What would he say if she told him she wanted to put aside her Harvard Business School education and bake?

She could hear her father's humorless laugh in the recesses of her mind. It was a stupid idea. It wouldn't be the first time she had broached the subject. But Charles Coopersmith always seemed to go deaf when she talked about a career change.

Right now everything was in order in the Coopersmith universe: Claudia was married to a man their father had all but hand-picked, and Caroline was in line to step into her father's role of senior partner when he retired.

A knot formed in her stomach at the mere thought. There was nothing she could do about it right now. That's why having a one-night stand with the best man at her sainted sister's wedding—a man of whom her father would never approve—was as close as she would come to defying him.

She tried to shrug off the inner voice calling her a coward. But it didn't really matter, did it? She knew in her gut that when she left the sanctuary of the bathroom, she would find the bed empty. Drew would've taken advantage of her absence to take his leave, and she would leave the fantasy of their one night behind and step back into real life.

So buck up. One night with Drew was exactly what you signed up for. This is how you wanted it to end.

She gave her reflection one last once-over. The foggy bathroom mirror reflected back a soft-focus image of a woman who looked a bit too hopeful to return to an empty bed. She ran her fingers

through her damp hair, pushing the errant chestnut strands away from her face. Tightening the
sash of the bathrobe, she opened the collar just
a little bit so that the right amount of cleavage
showed.

She turned out the light before she opened the
door, standing in the pitch-dark for a moment
to gather herself. She heard a distant door slam;
someone moving around in the room upstairs; the
distant resonance of a toilet flushing, a shower
starting. The symphony of hotel sounds set over
the reverb of her own breathing.

*All right, come on. You can't stay in here for-
ever.* Slowly, she turned the doorknob and stepped
into the dimly lit bedchamber.

The first thing to come into focus was her
bridesmaid dress, lying in a crumpled heap on
the floor. Next, a trail of various articles of un-
derclothing and men's clothing—

Her gaze zagged to the bed, where a mound
in the bed verified that Drew was still there. She
froze, uncertain of what to do. Should she get back
in bed or get dressed?

So much for avoiding the awkward morning-
after dance.

When Caroline's gaze adjusted to the low light,
the bridal bouquet, which lay on the nightstand,

came into focus. Perched precariously on the edge of the table, its bloodred roses were now drooping and showing their age. However, the blunt, thorn-free stems, chopped to uniform perfection and bound tightly in virginal, white satin ribbon, were still perfectly in place.

None of those roses could possibly break free from the pack. Now, if that wasn't a metaphor for the Coopersmith family way…

In Caroline's mind, a vision flashed of herself growing old and used up but still toeing the line at Coopersmith & Bales. All the blood drained from her head.

Drew stirred. His hand went up to his face, and he scrubbed his eyes before he propped himself up on his elbow.

"Good morning." His voice was a hoarse rasp. He eyed her up and down, and the last traces of bravado she had been full of last night vanished, like someone deadheading roses.

"Good morning." Her words slipped out on a whisper.

Grasping the lapels of her robe, she held them together, as if she were all modesty and virtue.

Oh, God, help me. It was too late for that now—too late for help or for modesty and virtue.

Drew patted the empty side of the bed next to him. "Come here."

It took a couple of beats to unstick her bare feet from the floor, but finally she forced her legs to move. She perched primly on the edge of the bed next to him, her hands in her lap. Her gaze again landed on the bridal bouquet, but she redirected it to Drew.

He looked so darn sexy lying there on his side, propped up on his elbow, the sheet pulled up to his waist, barely covering his hipbones. His biceps bulged and his broad shoulders looked a mile wide. She swallowed around the angst that was blocking her airway.

"Do you want some coffee?" she offered, finally finding her voice, then cringing at the inane question.

"No thanks." His hand was on her back, kneading her shoulder through the soft terry of the robe. "That's not what I'm in the mood for just now."

Without another word, he reached out and ran a finger along her jawline, down her neck, to the collar of her robe.

In one firm motion, he pulled her on top of him. And coffee completely lost its appeal.

* * *

"Tell me everything, and don't you dare skip a single detail," demanded Pepper Merriweather.

Caroline and Pepper had been best friends for as far back as they both could remember. Tonight they sat at Caroline's kitchen table, sharing a bottle of pinot noir and some to-die-for parmesan spinach dip Pepper had commandeered from the kitchen of Celebrations, Inc.

They'd settled in with a spread of crudités and crackers, and Pepper was obviously expecting the details of Caroline's time with Drew to be the main course.

Seeing as how they always told each other everything—stories about first boyfriends, first kisses, first heartbreaks, first and last dates—Caroline was having a hard time coming up with diversionary tactics. Because Caroline wasn't so eager to share the story of her first one-night stand.

She wasn't embarrassed. On the contrary, she was rather proud that for once she had not bowed to fear and had taken what she wanted. Not to mention the fact that it had happened with a guy like Drew Montgomery. That they'd spent all of Sunday morning in bed. Later they'd gone to brunch and had played together all day, until he'd dropped her off at home.

When was the last time she had *played?*

She had shared the surface points with Pepper. It was the more intimate details she was keeping closer to her chest.

Really, the only reason she and Pepper were having this conversation was that Pepper had said she'd seen Caroline and Drew dancing at the wedding Saturday night…and then she had seen the two of them leave together. Pepper tended to have a special kind of radar for things like that.

Now here Caroline was with her friend on Monday evening, sharing a bottle of wine, Pepper getting bolder and more insistent with each sip. The vaguer the answers Caroline gave, the more Pepper demanded the details.

The truth was, Caroline felt sort of like Cinderella having been to the ball, having danced with the prince all night, and now her coach had turned back into a pumpkin. Like Cinderella, she wanted more, despite the pact that she had made with herself that it would be just one night. But one night had turned into the next day, and pretty soon that pact she had made with herself was falling through the porch cracks as Drew kissed her good-night just before midnight.

So, now pactless and wanting more, she wasn't sure how Drew felt.

When he left, he had not promised he'd call. Caroline had convinced herself that that was a good thing. Because if he'd said it, she would've gotten her hopes up, only to have them dashed when he did not follow through.

Instead, he had not said it, and here she sat uncertain and vulnerable with her hopes up anyway.

Oh, God, what made me think I could have a one-night stand?

She dug her nails into her palms and reminded herself that it was what it was. She had wanted one perfect night with a guy who was perfectly imperfect for her. One night to release all the wedding stress and then she would return to her regularly scheduled life, which had no room for ongoing romance.

Because of that, she did not dare try to find her prince or hope that her prince would care enough to find her again—although Drew did know where she lived, and she already knew he made no pretense of being Prince Charming.

Well, okay, he'd earned the *charming* part. That was part of the reason she did not feel like dishing the details with her friend.

Pepper picked up the bottle of pinot noir and refilled Caroline's wineglass. That was an unspoken signal, and Caroline knew that in exactly four... three...two...one...

"Never in a million years would I have picked out a guy like him for you. But good for you, honey." She pushed Caroline's glass toward her and then clinked it with her own. "Cheers! I mean, if *I'd* been paired up with him, I would've gone for him myself. But it was obvious that he only had eyes for you."

Caroline smiled and shrugged as she sipped her wine, racking her brain for something— anything—to change the subject.

Too late.

"Now, I know y'all spent the night together," Pepper said, "but the burning question is, *when* are you going to see him again?"

There was a sparkle in Pepper's eyes that hinted that her doing such a thing would be pure decadence...and maybe even highly recommended.

Caroline tried to act nonchalant, despite the heat she felt rising in her cheeks. "I don't know," she answered truthfully. "I guess that remains to be seen."

Pepper straightened in her chair as if Caroline had just revealed the juiciest secret of all. "So that means you *would* see him again?"

Pepper cocked her head to the side, holding her wineglass midair.

"Well, why wouldn't I?"

Pepper blinked and looked little stunned. "But you want to see him again, right?"

Caroline sipped her wine, buying time. She rolled the liquid around on her tongue, savoring its cherries, plums and earthiness.

Being put on the spot by Pepper sort of had the same effect as flipping a coin for an answer—in that flash of seconds before fate decided the answer, she knew what she wanted in her heart of hearts.

Yes. She did want to see him again. They'd had a fabulous time together. A truly fabulous time. No one was more surprised by this than she was. He'd been sweet and gentle and interesting. What was more, he seemed genuinely interested in her.

He would call.

Wouldn't he?

Oh, God, what if he didn't call?

Drew spent way too many hours in the office, but long hours were the nature of his job as editor-in-chief of the *Dallas Journal of Business and Development*.

After taking three days off for the wedding and

spending all day Sunday with Caroline, he faced the age-old problem when he returned to work on Monday: his head just wasn't in the game. He hadn't been able to stop thinking about Caroline since he'd left her at the door after kissing her goodbye last night.

Even so, that morning, he'd hit the ground running—albeit with a smile on his face—and had not stopped all day.

Now, his computer screen glowed in the dusk of his dimly lit office. An article that one of the reporters had written about the opening of a new credit union in the area stared back at him blankly, and all he could think about was that at this time last night, he'd been with Caroline.

Come on, damn it. Focus on work.

Drew narrowed his gaze at his screen, redoubling his effort. It was stuffy in his closed office despite the cool October weather. Too bad he couldn't open a window and let in some fresh air. But the one window in his shoebox-size second-floor office was strictly for show and not function.

He got up and opened his office door instead. The newsroom was quiet. Since it was after eight, all the cubicles were empty, including the one that belonged to managing editor Bia Anderson. Since Bia and the staff had worked double time in his absence, he had intended to work extra hard for the next four days to pull the rest of the week's edition together. He'd sent her home early. He was alone in the office.

The newsroom was eerily silent. The faint smell of coffee hung in the air, mingling with newsprint and something else that was unique to the office. Drew liked to think it was the smell of ambition.

He made his way to the small kitchenette, and for a moment he thought about putting on another pot of coffee, but he dismissed the idea when he saw that someone had already cleaned up the coffee station. No use in dirtying it up again today, even though he was going to be there a while. He settled on a glass of cold water from the cooler next to the coffeemaker and made his way back to his desk.

Since the *Dallas Journal of Business and Development* hit the stands on Friday—a strategy designed to allow the *Journal* a slim margin to scoop the competition—the daily paper's special tabloid-size business section, which ran on Mondays—Drew's week began on Friday and ended on Thursday.

That meant he worked most weekends. Technically, Monday was midweek for him. After taking off Friday, Saturday and Sunday, he should have been way behind schedule. But since Bia had done such a beautiful job handling the first three days of the week, it wasn't so bad.

Of course, there were still things that only he could do…in addition to editing the handful of articles that were just coming across his desk.

Being the editor-in-chief of the newspaper meant he had to be disciplined and had to keep everyone else on track. He shifted in his chair, squeezed his eyes shut for a moment as he took a long drink of water. He opened his eyes again.

The *Journal* may have been a small operation, but Drew ran a tight ship and expected nothing less of everyone else.

Yet, even as he resumed editing the credit union article, his thoughts drifted to the events of the past weekend.

It had been a long time since he'd been distracted like this, and all he could think was, *Damn, she was worth the wait.* Even though he had no idea he'd been waiting. Or that he'd been waiting for her.

This thought helped him power through the article. He finished it, saved the changes and exited out. Pushing back from his desk, he acknowledged that it was time to take a break more substantial than getting a glass of water. He'd worked through dinner. So maybe a break would leave him better off in the long run.

He picked up the phone and dialed Caroline's number. It rang four times. He thought it was going to voice mail when she picked up.

"Hello?" Her voice sounded like heaven to his ears.

"Hi, I have this tuxedo hanging in my closet. And I have this really hideous pumpkin-colored tie hanging there with it. I understand that you might know of someone who has an outfit—preferably a dress—that might complement it or at least make it look good."

Her laugh was low and sexy.

"I think I know just the person you have in mind."

The sound of her voice made him smile. He leaned back in his chair, and for the first time since he'd left her at her front door last night, he felt the tension melt out of his shoulders.

"So, where besides a wedding does one wear such unsightly pumpkin getups?" he asked.

"That depends on the pumpkins involved," she said. "Pumpkins are always welcome at the farmers' markets. This time of year, they're frequently spotted in the produce aisle of the grocery store.

Or for the really adventurous, they've been known to frequent ravioli and various pies and pastries. But that's not for the everyday pumpkin; definitely not for the faint of heart."

"That's very good to know," he said. "So, you're not faint of heart, are you?"

"Me? No. Not me. Not at all."

"Did not think so. I didn't take you for that sort of girl."

"What's that supposed to mean?" Her voice wavered a little bit.

So she wasn't as tough as she was pretending to be. Quick-witted, yes. But not tough.

"That's my lame way of asking you if you'd like to go to the farmers' market with me Thursday night. We can put on our hideous pumpkin outfits and have a scandalous night on the town."

"The farmers' market is only open on Saturday mornings. I don't think we can have a night on the town there."

"You're not going to make this easy, are you?"

"No. I'm definitely not easy, if that's what you were thinking."

He smiled. She wasn't exactly what he would call bristly, but he could tell he'd struck a nerve. Of course she wasn't easy; she was damn irresistible.

"Then how about simply going out to dinner with me Thursday night?"

After a few beats of silence, she said, "I'd like that very much." Her voice was soft again.

He heard muffled background voices over the line.

"Is someone there with you?"

"Yes. Did you meet my friend Pepper Merriweather? She was at the wedding."

Of course he remembered Pepper. Everyone in the Southeast knew Pepper Merriweather. "Right. Yes, I did meet her. Her dad is Texas Star Energy, right?"

Caroline laughed. "Yes, though I'd never really thought of him that way. But yes, I guess in a sense he *is* Texas Star Energy."

"I've interviewed her father before for the paper."

He paused, waiting for her to react. It was an interesting dynamic. With a certain set of Dallas's business elite, the *Journal* had a reputation for being reckless and socially impudent, which, in common man's terms, meant Drew published the cold, hard truth. He'd butted heads with Harris Merriweather and some of the higher-ups at Texas Star when Drew had asked questions that, for some reason, they did not want to answer.

It was his duty to inform the public. It was also his job to ensure the stories he published were true and unbiased. The only way he could achieve that goal was to talk to people in the know. People who were willing to talk and tell him the truth. When sources stonewalled, it sent up red flags. Those red flags only encouraged Drew to push harder. Still, with Texas Star, he got nowhere.

While Caroline and her friend Pepper moved in those elite Dallas society circles, Caroline seemed no more one of them than Drew was. Maybe that's why they'd had such a strong connection. Whatever the reason, he couldn't remember the last time he'd connected with a woman on so many levels.

"So Thursday, then. I'll pick you up at seven."

It was going to be a long three days.

Chapter Three

Drew's distraction at work was a testament to how much Caroline had gotten to him. Apparently, his attention deficit was also obvious to his coworkers.

On Thursday morning, Bia knocked on his door and stuck her head inside his office. "What's up, Drew?"

"Business as usual," he said, not looking up from his computer.

"Got a minute?"

"Umm…" He finished what he was doing on

the computer before he glanced up. "Sure. Come on in."

Bia shut the office door. Tucking one leg underneath her, she settled herself on a chair across from his desk.

"How late were you here last night?" she asked.

"I left around two." He continued typing as he talked so not to waste time.

She gasped. "Two in the morning?"

"No, I left at two yesterday afternoon." He looked up at her and scrubbed a hand over his face. "Of course two in the morning."

"All right, grouchy. Obviously someone needs a nap."

He had not meant to bite her head off. It was already four-thirty. He'd hoped to put this week's edition to bed by five, but thanks to some glitches, he was running behind. "Sorry, B, I'm just trying to finish up here. Didn't mean to snap at you."

Bia nodded. "Something else besides this week's edition is on your mind. I can tell. Want to talk about it?"

She was perceptive, that was for sure. It was a quality that made her a great reporter and an even better editor. But he really did not want her digging in his personal life.

"What makes you think I have something other than work on my mind?"

She quirked a brow at him. "Maybe the way you seem to be in an extra big hurry to get the paper out this week."

"What's wrong with that?" he asked.

"Who said there was anything wrong with it? It's just out of character for you."

Drew tried to keep his face neutral. When Bia got a whiff that she was onto something, she read all the signs and signals until she had enough to substantiate her hunch.

"Do you have a date tonight?" she asked.

Drew looked away and started working on his computer again. Probably the wrong move—

"You do. You have a date! Who is she, Drew?"

Oh, hell. He really didn't want to bring his personal life to the office. He'd learned the pitfalls of that the hard way when he and the woman he'd almost married both worked at the *Colorado Journal of Business and Development,* before they were both promoted to posts as editors-in-chief of different papers. He got the Dallas paper. Joan got the *Seattle Journal.*

When it became clear that one of them would have to compromise their career, it became fodder for the office gossip mill. Everyone was speculating on which one would give up the dream job for the preservation of their relationship. In the end, they sacrificed their future together. To this day, they remained good friends and even better colleagues, calling on each other for professional advice and sharing a good-natured rivalry concerning circulation and notable scoops.

After they broke up, Drew vowed to leave his personal life at home. As the editor-in-chief, it would be unprofessional to date one of his staff. In fact, Drew had instituted a no-dating policy among the staff of his paper. It just kept things cleaner. No jealousy, no bitter breakups to add to the tension of an industry that was already stressful by nature.

"Drew? You are out of it today." Something bounced off his temple. It only took a second to realize Bia had wadded up a piece of paper and thrown it at him.

"Seriously?" He tried to frown at her but ended up smiling in spite of himself.

"You're always the first one here in the morning and last one to leave," said Bia. "Go on. Get out of here. This edition is almost done. I'll see it through until the files are emailed off to the printer."

Drew's smile faded. He knew he was looking at

her as if she had two heads. Did she really think he would cut out early on drop day? Especially after taking a three-day weekend?

"No, thanks. I got this. I can call and let her know I'm going to be a few minutes late.

Bia whistled. "I knew it." Her voice was triumphant.

Drew cocked a brow at her to make it clear he'd let that bit of info slip on purpose.

"The news that, yes, indeed, I have a date does not need to be leaked to the rest of the newsroom."

"On one condition," Bia challenged.

"No conditions," Drew countered.

"*One* condition. Do not be late. That is not a way to impress her. For that matter, you don't have to permanently block out every single Thursday on your calendar from now till the end of time," she said. "We're just waiting on the Sugar Hill story. If you'd trust me just a little to demonstrate that I can pull it off, which is what you've been training me to do, we could start switching off late Thursdays. And you could get out of here early tonight and go see whoever it is that's had you preoccupied since you got back from the wedding."

He drummed his fingers on the desk, thinking. She was right—in more than one way. For the better part of a year, he had been training Bia for an editorship. She could handle it. If she got into a bind, she could call him. But there wouldn't really be a bind because almost everything was done except for the late-breaking Sugar Hill scoop. They were waiting to verify a few facts that would allow them to scoop the daily paper.

Then again, he could've waited one more night—or at least until after the paper was put to bed—to see Caroline again.

Hell, he had not wanted to wait. And Bia was right: being late wasn't the best way to make a good first impression. So why rush the Sugar Hill story that Jeff Thomas was ironing out?

"Jeff just sent me the preliminary copy," Drew said. "That's what I was looking at before you knocked. Do you think you can edit and format it?"

"Absolutely."

"Okay, I'll email it to you. He shortened it a little bit, but I think we probably need to cut it by at least a hundred and fifty words. Maybe a little more, depending on how much additional stuff he needs to add."

Bia nodded.

Drew attached the file to an email and sent it to her. "If you could just give it a look and see where you think he could trim it that would be a lot of help."

"Sure," Bia said. "I was looking over the profile on George Hildebrand for next week. Soon as I put this one to bed, I'll get right to that one.

It was close to 5:45 by the time Drew was finally able to extract himself from the office. He had an hour and fifteen minutes to go home, shower and shave before he picked up Caroline at seven. He made record time. Soon, the two of them were walking into Bistro Saint-Germain in downtown Celebration.

It was an upscale spot with floor-to-ceiling glass doors that folded open so that the dining room spilled out onto the patio and sidewalk outside the restaurant. The tables were covered with crisp white linens and sported small votive candles and vases hosting single red rosebuds.

As they approached the maitre d' stand, soft strains of a jazz quartet and muted conversation buzzed in the air. The bistro was hopping on this fine Thursday night. The place obviously wasn't hurting for business, as was evidenced by the small crowd that waited at the bar. Drew was glad he'd made a reservation.

As they waited for the hostess to gather menus,

Caroline leaned in and asked, "Where's your pumpkin tie?"

He looked down at his chest and feigned surprise.

"Probably the same place as your pumpkin dress," he said.

She smiled. "Well, I hope they're having a wonderful time. Wherever they are tonight, I'm sure they make a handsome couple."

He gazed at her, taking in her emerald-green eyes and the striking contrast they made paired with her chestnut hair. Her lush lips—the top lip just a little fuller than the bottom—and the way her delicate jaw curved into her slender neck. "I'm sure they do."

As the hostess seated them at a table for two in a quiet corner of the garden patio, he realized he'd never believed in love at first sight…until now.

He'd fallen in love with Caroline the moment he'd first set eyes on her.

It had not been that way with Joan. In fact, with Joan, he'd believed there was no such thing as a soul mate or destiny. His philosophy had conformed to the idea that people were too damaged or too busy or too self-absorbed to make room in their souls for one perfect mate. Love had always been about two damaged people finding each other at the precise moment in their lives when their flaws and needs were arranged in a pattern where they could mesh and a relationship could grow.

Not very romantic, he admitted.

He and Joan had fallen together in the workplace and had given the best of themselves to the job. They made no pretense of romance. Their flaws had mingled and aligned in the residual of what really mattered to them. When their needs shifted, their new patterns didn't fit, and everything ended.

Then he met Caroline and his beliefs tipped on their axis.

The crazy part was he did not even know her beyond the ethereal, beyond the fact that she was damn good at making him feel equal parts electrically charged and at ease around her. There was something magical here.

Here was a woman he'd met a week ago, and already he found himself daydreaming about a future with her. Those daydreams seemed more real than anything in his past.

After ordering a bottle of wine, he gazed at her across the table.

"So tell me about yourself."

He grimaced. He had not meant to make it

sound so formal, and he racked his brain for a way to reframe his comment, to make it more personal, less…professional.

"I don't mean to sound like I'm interviewing you. I just want to know you better. Because I don't know much about you except that your sister just married my best friend, you seem to have an aversion to the color pumpkin and you seem to love champagne. Who is Caroline Coopersmith?"

She gazed at him across the table, pondering the question.

Who was she? Well, that was a loaded question.

Mercifully, the server brought the wine and went through the tasting formalities, buying her time to think.

Who am I?

When they were alone again, she said, "And you say you're *not* interviewing me?"

"Nope." He shook his head and then narrowed his eyes and looked at her for a long moment as they clinked wineglasses. The awareness took her breath away.

"I want to know more about you, that's all. What makes you tick? What ticks you off? What were you like when you were a kid? How many weddings have you been in?"

Her mouth dropped open. "What?"

Weddings, or morning after the weddings? Like there really was a question about which he meant. The way he smiled confirmed that she had correctly read the implication in his words.

She clucked her tongue at him and wrinkled her nose.

He waved away the question. "Just kidding about the weddings."

Maybe so, but, she if he brought it up there was a grain of truth in his teasing. "Well, for the record, this is the only 'wedding' I've ever been in."

She held his gaze, wanting to make sure he understood exactly what she meant. That she did not make a habit of sleeping around.

He nodded. "I guess that's really none of my business, is it? But I…I like you. And I guess I just wanted to know.…" His eyes searched her face and she thought he looked relieved. Just then something seemed to shift between them…in a good way, and it made her feel a little vulnerable.

He liked her. That was a good thing. A very good thing. She looked away and then quickly looked back at him. She had read somewhere that that was a way to flirt. The coy act of *I'm not looking at you; oh, wait, yes I am* was supposed to send a message that a woman was interested in a man. Just in case he'd missed the earlier clues.

Ugh, she was terrible at things like this. It certainly had not been any easier when she was pretending to be a woman who lived fast and loose. So maybe that was all the more reason that she should just be herself.

"Well, okay then. To answer your question, I'm afraid I don't lead a very exciting life. I'm a financial analyst by day and I bake cakes by night. So basically you might say that my life amounts to counting beans and baking. Tons of fun, I know."

"In that order?" he asked.

She narrowed her gaze at him. "I don't understand."

He smiled. "So you're a bean counter who bakes cakes. It's beans before dessert, right?"

"I guess so." She laughed. "Yes, unfortunately right now, it is beans before dessert. But it wouldn't be that way if I had my way."

"Really?"

"You know what they say—life is short." He smiled. "You should eat dessert first."

She laughed. "I like the way you think."

She raised her wine goblet and they clinked glasses. A loaded silence ensued as they sipped the sauvignon blanc.

"But still, I want to know about you," he said. "Beyond beans and dessert. Because that's not the essence of you. What are you passionate about?"

Passionate? The word made her a little uneasy, and she knew she needed to get over the fact that she had slept with him *before* their first date. He was still here. He was interested. She needed to quit overthinking things.

At a loss for words, she swirled the wine in her goblet, watching the pale gold liquid, illuminated by the candlelight, flow down the inside of the glass. She was struck by Drew's curiosity, wondering when the last time was that someone had wanted to know about her…her thoughts and feelings. What mattered to her. Her life had revolved around Coopersmith & Bales for so long, which meant that most of her moves had been dictated by her father and his business partner, Richard Bales. They'd certainly never taken the time to ask about her. Perhaps it was the nature of the accounting business, which was pretty formulaic. Not much room for gray areas or opinion.

Because of that, Caroline had grown used to listening, plugging in the numbers where they belonged. She could do her job in her sleep. It was all pretty rote.

A.J., Pepper and Sydney James, another friend,

always cared about her thoughts and feelings—although, come to think of it, they were usually the ones who did most of the talking. As the most introspective of the quartet of friends, Caroline was the more content listening and dispensing advice, much in the same way she prescribed accounting advice to Coopersmith & Bales's clients.

So…passion? What *was* she passionate about? This was a chance for a clean state with Drew. A do-over. A chance for him to know the real her. Whatever she told him now was how he would see her.

Beyond the firm and Celebrations, Inc., and baking, what was she all about? Beyond cakes and confections and the touch of a man, what did she hunger for?

Drew's question gave her pause, because obviously she had never pondered this herself. And why had she not? Why had she never asked herself this?

"Caroline?" He reached across the table and put his hand on hers. A cool breeze blew across the patio, and the air smelled of fall and a mélange of delicious food smells coming from the restaurant.

"Yes, umm…I guess I can't say that I've really pondered what I'm passionate about. Not in so many words. I suppose I've never really taken the time. My job at Coopersmith & Bales is pretty demanding. And I bake a lot for Celebrations, Inc. So, perhaps baking is my passion?"

Lame. That sounded lame. Maybe if they got serious enough she would introduce him to her cat. Wow, cakes and cats. She sounded like an eighty-five-year-old spinster. Maybe she should've quit while she was ahead and let him think of her as the adventurous vixen.

"Celebrations, Inc.? What's that?"

"You haven't heard of Celebrations, Inc., the catering company?" She feigned surprise.

"Rings a bell," he said. "Tell me more."

She shrugged. "It's a relatively new catering company. My friend A. J. Sherwood-Antonelli started it earlier this year. In fact, at one time, A.J. worked right here at Bistro Saint-Germain as the sous chef. A couple of friends and I are silent partners in Celebrations, Inc.—Pepper, who was over when you called the other night, another friend of ours, Sydney James, and I all invested in the company. Sometimes we help out A.J. if she's in a bind…and sometimes I supply Celebrations, Inc. with desserts to serve, but it's definitely my part-time job. Although A.J. has been relentless about trying to get us to come on board full-time."

"So, life is sweet, huh?" he said.

What? "Uh, yeah, life is…sweet. That was a bad pun, Drew. Is stand-up comedy your secret passion?"

"Touché." He raised his glass to her. "So, tell me a secret about you."

"Beyond my fierce wedding after-parties? What's there to say?"

She couldn't believe she had said that. But the look on his face made her glad she had. It was *that*—what she saw in his expression and the fact that she could say something like that to him rather than just think it—*that* was a case in point that illustrated this…this…*thing* they shared. A chemistry that bubbled up between them and urged her to step outside of her shell and take chances. In a way, *that* was passion.

"Somehow, I get the feeling there's a lot more to you than the woman I met at our wedding after-party."

She melted a little inside.

He had the most incredible eyes. They were a dark brown—the color of flourless chocolate torte. Eyes that she could lose herself in. And his lips were even more delicious. Her gaze dropped to his mouth. She had the urge to lean in closer and taste them. Right there in the restaurant, in the middle of downtown Celebration.

Instead, she said, "Okay, here's something more. From me to you. I'm really glad the after-party wasn't a one-time engagement. I'm really glad you called. That's my secret."

There was heartrending tenderness in his smile. A sensuous light passed between them, and Caroline was filled with longing.

"I am, too," he said.

Of course, leave it to the server to choose that precise moment to approach the table to tell them about the specials of the night.

After they ordered, she tried to shift the conversation to him and his passions, but Drew pressed her for more.

After Drew paid the bill, the two of them headed toward the car. Caroline was hyperaware of him as they walked side by side. The pressure of his hand on the small of her back was more personal than if he'd simply walked beside her, but not quite as intimate as if he'd held her hand or put his arm around her. Were they starting over and taking things slow? Whatever they were doing, she liked it.

They walked a while in companionable silence, until Drew broke the quiet.

"Do you think you'll ever leave Coopersmith & Bales to go full-time at Celebrations?"

She smiled, debating whether it was a good idea to answer one way or another, since she had not made up her mind completely.

"In due time, I suppose. I hope. Although some of us will probably leap sooner than others. Sydney is convinced that she's going to be out of a job soon. So she's planning on cutting bait before things get any weirder."

"Where does she work?"

"Texas Star Energy."

"What's going on?" he asked.

"She said there have been some strange things with the quarterly reports and—"

She flinched, remembering she was talking to the editor-in-chief of a business newspaper.

Giving herself a mental shake, she reminded herself of damage caused by loose lips. She was beginning to see a pattern: a couple of glasses of liquid courage mixed with the viral potency of Drew Montgomery tended to make her throw common sense and good judgment out the window.

"Of course, everything I've just said is off the record, right?"

"Caroline?" Before he could answer her, a voice called her name. She turned to see Doris Grady, a friend of her mother's, waving at her as she crossed the street.

"Hello, Doris."

"I thought that was you," said the older woman. "How lovely to see you this evening, dear."

Doris was eying Drew, obviously liking what she saw and anticipating an introduction.

"Doris, this is my friend Drew Montgomery. Drew, Mrs. Doris Grady."

The older woman offered her hand.

"Why yes, I remember you. You were the best man in Claudia's wedding this weekend."

The woman had a sharp memory. Then again, a guy as handsome as Drew was pretty darn unforgettable.

Drew took her hand and gave it a squeeze-shake, which made Doris swoon a little. "It's very nice to see you again," Drew said, his delivery perfect and charming, matching the perfectly charming gesture he'd delivered earlier. Now he had her rapt, hanging on his words. This man had a way with the ladies, and he obviously knew it.

Doris beamed, eyeing the two of them. "I had

no idea you two were an item. Or did the romance of the wedding bring you together? I just love weddings. Don't you?"

Oh, boy. This wasn't the time to explain exactly what they were to each other. How could she, when she didn't even know herself?

She glanced up at Drew. He was staring down at her—she had not realized just how tall he was. Or maybe it was that she was feeling a little small and unsure of herself at the moment thanks to the careless Texas Star comment. Surely, he wouldn't… She had to make sure he understood that anything said when they were together was off-limits.

"I am a lucky guy to have such a beautiful woman on my arm, aren't I?"

Drew looped his arm through Caroline's and pulled her in close.

Doris swooned again. So did Caroline…just a little bit…silently, on the inside. Drew's diversion of the subject had done the trick. At least long enough to distract the older woman until her husband, who had probably been parking the car, joined her.

"Harold, I want you to meet Drew Montgomery," she said. "Or have you met him already? He was the best man in Claudia and Kyle's wedding on Saturday. Remember?"

The two shook hands, but before her husband had a chance to answer, Doris turned sparkling eyes on Caroline. "Are the two of you next? If so, I'd better get an invitation to the wedding."

She hoped Drew would come up with another distraction, but when she looked up at him, waiting for him to take the diversionary ball and run with it, he just smiled as if saying, *It's your turn.*

Caroline cleared her throat. "Of course you will be invited to my wedding, when that day comes. But it will probably be a while." *If ever,* she thought. "Tonight, I'm just showing Drew around Celebration."

"Oh, are you from out of town, dear?" Doris asked.

"No, not really. I live in Dallas. I just haven't had the opportunity to spend much time in Celebration."

"From Dallas, you say?" Harold spoke for the first time. He seemed to be sizing up Drew. "Would your name happen to be *Andrew* Montgomery?"

"Yes, my full name is Andrew."

"You wouldn't have anything to do with that

Dallas Journal of Business and Development,
would you?"

"Yes, I'm the editor of the paper."

Harold's eyes flashed. "I thought so. Son, if
my wife weren't here right now, I'd deck you flat.
Because of a story your rag did on my company,
the IRS was all over us. Come on, Doris, let's
go. Now."

Caroline stood there stunned as Doris shot her
an apologetic look and then trotted off after her
husband.

"Well, I had no idea you were infamous," Caroline said. "You just keep getting more and more
interesting by the minute."

He blew out an audible breath. "That's one of
the hazards of my job. Sometimes people take
issue with what we publish. But we're fair and
unbiased in our reporting."

He put his hand on her back as if to resume
their walk to the car, but Caroline stayed rooted
to the spot.

"Drew, I'm not going to be able to sleep tonight
if I don't get this off my chest. Earlier what I said
about Sydney leaving Texas Star...well, she hasn't
left yet and she very well may not. So I hope you
won't take what I said out of context."

He frowned. "I don't take things out of context. I report the facts. If there's no story there, then there's no story there."

Chapter Four

On Friday, Drew sat in his office at his desk with a year's worth of Texas Star quarterly reports spread out in front of him.

At the top of the stack was the most recent report, released last week. He hadn't had time to go over it before because of the wedding and coming back to dive into the weekly deadline.

Now that he was at the start of a brand-new week for the paper, he was devouring the report with interest. At first glance nothing seemed amiss, but he couldn't shake what Caroline had said at dinner last night about her friend Sydney, who worked for Texas Star, saying something weird was going on with the quarterly reports.

Of course she had also asked him to keep what she had said off the record. And why shouldn't she expect that? They were on a date. It wasn't an interview—despite how they'd joked that it felt like he'd been interviewing her.

All night, he'd struggled with whether to reopen the Texas Star investigation. As the editor-in-chief, he would be remiss if he did not give the files one more look. He'd started looking into the energy conglomerate three months ago after a profile of Texas Star CEO Harris Merriweather left Drew scratching his head. Each time he'd asked Merriweather to explain the company's complicated financials in layman's terms, Merriweather came back with a glib response or threw up some sort of diversion to skirt the issue.

Even when Drew asked Merriweather to explain exactly how Texas Star made its money, Merriweather talked in riddles. When pressed, the CEO shot back a condescending, "I don't have time to explain the theories of economics 101 to you. What kind of a business newspaper editor are you if you can't decipher a simple financial statement?"

As much as Drew hated to admit it, Merriweather's roadblocks worked. They ran the Harris Merriweather profile and cooled the investigation after inquiries to a handful of stock and credit analysts admitted that while Texas Star stock was indeed considered Wall Street's golden ticket, even they were hard-pressed to explain the financials or exactly how the company made its money.

After getting responses such as, "When you crack their code, will you let me know?" And, "Well, yeah, I'm rather intimidated by that stock. It's doing well, but if something happens, say if they can't meet their numbers, as high as the valuation is, that stock is going to crater."

Drew felt as if he were dealing with the Riddle of the Sphinx. He had a gut feeling that if he solved the riddle there might be a story—and judging by the way Merriweather was blustering and blowing him off, Drew guessed there was a substantial story. The flipside to the Sphinx analogy was that all who failed to solve the riddle were destroyed.

That renewed challenge was the impetus that drove Drew to take one more look. Not what Caroline had said at dinner last night. And if he believed that, he was lying to himself.

He put down the report he was scrutinizing and, unfortunately, with which he was getting nowhere fast. He rubbed his eyes, realizing too late that he probably should've mentioned to Caroline that he had an ongoing…fascination with her friend's father's company.

He also wished he would've asked her if Harris Merriweather was always such a bastard. Nah, on second thought, asking that question probably wouldn't have been a good move. But reassuring her that he wasn't investigating because of what she said would've been smart.

He'd tell her. Well, he would if it looked like he was getting any closer to cracking the Texas Star code. First and foremost, he needed to learn how to separate himself from work. Over the years, he'd become such a workaholic it had ruined some relationships. He guessed it was the nature of the beast, aka his job. Case in point: how Harold Grady had been ready to deck him last night over the story Drew had published. Such was the life of a journalist. Sometimes reporting the truth made people mad.

Texas Star was one of the financial pillars of the Dallas community. It supported charities, and the corporation gave a big boost to the Dallas economy—not to mention they had a worldwide reputation for excellence. There probably wasn't a story here. So, the off-the-record agreement Caroline had asked for was a moot point. Employees of large businesses got disgruntled every day.

Still, the reporter in him couldn't rest until he had exhausted all angles and proved that the potential story was a dead end.

A knock on his door drew him from his thoughts. Bia stood in the threshold with a stack of papers in her hand. "Do you have a second?" she said.

"Sure, come on in. Have a seat. What's up?"

"I have the bio for the features here. It's the one written by the freelancer." She frowned. "I'm finding a lot of holes in it. I think it's too rough for us to run this week. Is there anything else we can put in its spot?"

"Is it that bad?" Drew asked.

Bia held out a piece of paper across the desk. "Read it and weep."

Drew waved her off. "Bounce it back to him and have him fill in the holes. Give me a few minutes to make a phone call or two, and I'll get a piece that we can run in its place."

"Sounds great." Bia stood up to go.

"Hold on just a second," Drew said. He picked up one of the Texas Star reports. "I'm looking at the Texas Star numbers again, trying to make sense of them. But they're still as convoluted as they always have been. Would you take the new report and give it a once-over? See if I'm missing anything?"

Bia put a hand on her hip.

"You're not going to let this go, are you?" She took the report and glanced at it. "You really think there's something here?"

Drew shrugged. "Based on what I just read, no. At face value, everything seems to line up."

He shook his head at his own doggedness. The phrase "beating a dead horse" came to mind. But that really was an awful analogy, wasn't it?

"You know, it's our job to read each organization's newest financial report. So, let's say that's why we're doing it. Sound good?"

Bia shrugged. "Sounds good to me. I'll look it over and let you know if I find anything."

Drew's call had been unexpected, and that made it all the more exciting. Caroline loved the way her stomach somersaulted when she saw Drew's name on the caller ID. And what she loved even more was the way her heart sang when she heard his voice on the line.

Thanks to him, the shadows had cleared and she woke up every morning with something to anticipate: a call, a text or some other reminder that he was in her life. That's why it was extra difficult when real life began to get in the way of their snow globe–perfect relationship.

That morning, he'd called wanting to see her that night, but she had promised A.J. twenty meringue-frosted coconut cakes with raspberry filling for the next day. With a heavy heart, she had declined his offer. Unfortunately, she couldn't even make a late dinner. Because once she got home from work, even if she ate on the fly, it was going to take her until three in the morning to bake the twenty cakes.

Drew had been understanding—apologetic, even, for the short notice—and they made a date for the weekend.

That's why the last thing she expected was for him to show up at her door with a bag of Chinese takeout and a smile that made her think things so sinful she felt as if she needed to do penance.

"What are you doing here?" She leaned in and kissed him hello, lingering a little to make sure that he understood what she really meant was *I'm so glad you're here.*

"I came to ask you a question," he said. "And to bring you dinner. I thought you might be too busy to eat."

"Well, aren't you just the—"

Food bag in one hand, he pulled her to him with the other. Their lips brushed. It was only a whisper of a kiss, but it made her heart pound and her brain say *oooh*. His lips tasted like peppermint and something indefinable—something potent and male.

She leaned in for another taste, and the whisper-kiss grew into a slow-burning passion that started with lips and hints of tongue, until he pulled her closer, turning his head ever so slightly and deepening their connection. She slid her arms around his neck, fisting her hands into his shirt collar, pulling him closer.

Losing herself in that kiss, she enjoyed how he made her feel—so alive and…wanton, craving his touch, his lips on her temple, her earlobe, her neck—

"Come inside," she said, pulling away, breathless.

He rested his forehead against hers. "I don't want to distract you from your work.

"Too late for that," she said. "Do you know how to bake a cake?"

"No, can't say I've ever tried."

"Do you want to learn?"

"Do I ever."

She pressed her finger to his lips. "Just as long

as you understand that sex in not part of tonight's recipe."

She straightened his collar, as if setting right his clothes right would set the tone for a chaste second date.

"Well, I did come with an ulterior motive, but I promise you it's not to seduce you."

"What?"

"I'll tell you about it over dinner," he said.

As they made their way into the kitchen, she thought, *Thank goodness this is date number two...wait, did this count as a date toward the three-date rule?*

More important, even if this *was* a date, would he come back for a third date after catching her looking like such a fright?

When she baked, she got comfortable. She had washed her face clean of the day's stress and makeup. She had pulled her hair back into a high ponytail. She had traded in her staid business suit for a decidedly dressed-down ensemble of an oversized T-shirt and sweat pants—old, faded, shrunken sweat pants that hit her midcalf and were more comfortable than just about anything she had ever worn.

She *never* let anyone see her dressed like this. For a split second, she panicked and thought about excusing herself to change clothes and fix herself up, but then she decided, *nope*. He'd come over unannounced. This was Caroline in real life, away from the halls of Coopersmith & Bales. If he couldn't handle it, well…

Wishing that she really were as brave as she was pretending to be, she handed him two plates. "Will you please put these on the table with the food?"

"Sure."

She gathered napkins, silverware and wineglasses—making an agreement with herself that she would only have one glass.

When they were settled at the table, the wine poured and the chicken with cashews and sautéed string beans dished up, he said, "Would you allow me to interview you and your friends for the business profile section of the *Journal?*"

Caroline froze, her fork midair. "Are you kidding? That would be wonderful! Really?"

He nodded. "Yes, really. The only catch is it has to be soon. We have a hole in this week's profile section. A freelancer did not come through with an assignment. Do you think you could arrange it for tomorrow? I was hoping to interview you and your friends. I'd bring a photographer to shoot photos of you at the Celebrations, Inc. office."

"Oh, my gosh, A.J. is just going to die when she hears about this. I'll call her right after we finish eating."

One of Drew's favorite parts of the job was when his interview inquiries made people happy. More often than not, that wasn't the case. But seeing Caroline smile and then learning that A.J., Pepper and Sydney had actually used the word *hero* when talking about him and how they were rearranging their schedules to accommodate an interview went a long way toward making up for the negativity.

When he arrived at the Celebrations, Inc. offices he didn't see Caroline's silver Acura parked out front. He and Caroline had agreed to meet there since they were coming from opposite sides of town.

The plan was to get the interview and photos done within an hour, as Caroline and Sydney had to get back to work. Simon, the *Journal*'s staff photographer, was coming from another job and would meet them there in about forty-five minutes.

Drew maneuvered his Mustang into a parking space. Grasping his notebook and a couple of pens, he headed up the flower-lined cobblestone walk to the office, which was housed in a store-front shop. From the looks of the place, at one time, it might have been two separate shops. Now it appeared that the catering company occupied the entire building.

A wooden front door featured a large, leaded Tiffany-style stained-glass panel of colorful flowers that formed an ornate wreath around cobalt glass that spelled out Celebrations, Inc., Catering. At the bottom of the door was a shiny brass kick plate that complemented the brass door handle.

Nice first impression.

It had been a long time since he'd gone out on an interview, even longer since he'd written a profile.

As the editor-in-chief, Drew usually did not write pieces like the business profiles, but obviously this was a special case, the exception to the rule. Caroline was becoming the exception to many of Drew's rules. The mere idea of that made him smile. That, and the change of work-related assignment felt good. Or maybe it was the anticipation of seeing Caroline in yet another environment. Last night, they'd baked cakes—twenty in all—until nearly two in the morning. If someone would've told him baking was as sexy as Caroline made it, he would've told them they were crazy.

In the past, he'd always equated baking with Grandma, or Betty Crocker or maybe even Sara Lee. But helping Caroline measure, sift and stir added new elements to it. After last night, he'd never look at flour and sugar quite the same way.

Of course, it had all been very chaste. Caroline wanted to slow down the physical dimension of their relationship for the time being. She was serious about what she called the "third-date rule." He respected that. No woman wanted to feel used, as if a guy only wanted her for one thing. He certainly had no intention of her being a friend with benefits. He wanted much more.

Although, despite their late night last night, tonight they'd planned on meeting for a late dinner after he wrote and filed the business profile on Celebrations.

Technically, *tonight* would be their third date. Maybe that's what had him smiling and in such a good mood today.

He pulled open the door and a cluster of ribbon-tied brass bells attached to the handle sounded. As he stepped through the threshold into the lobby, classical music played over a sound system. Two upholstered chairs stood in front of a reception desk that looked expensive and antique. The trio of furniture was arranged in the center of a Persian rug atop hardwood flooring. The decor lent an air of upscale sophistication to the establishment.

Based on his first impression, Drew was beginning to form the words for the article's lead paragraph when a petite blonde entered the lobby through a set of double doors he hadn't noticed behind the desk.

"You must be Drew," she said and extended her hand. Drew moved his notebook from his right hand to his left and accepted her firm but feminine grip. "I'm A.J. It's great to finally meet you. Caroline has said so many wonderful things about you."

Really? He smiled and hoped A.J. wasn't just being nice. Hell, when was the last time he'd worried about what someone thought? A long time ago.

"Nice to meet you, too," he said.

"Thanks so much for doing the profile on Celebrations, Inc. for the paper," A.J. said. "It will give us a tremendous boost."

"My pleasure. Thanks for making yourself available on such short notice. I have a photographer coming shortly."

"Good. Why don't you come back to the kitchen with me and I'll introduce you to Pepper and Sydney. Caroline's not here yet, but she will be soon."

He followed her through the doors into a large kitchen with stainless-steel counters and industrial appliances. The place was so clean, the metal seemed to gleam.

Two women were sitting at an island workstation in the middle of the kitchen. One of them he recognized as Pepper Merriweather. The other—a tall, thin brunette—he'd never seen before.

Both of the women stood, and that's when he noticed that the island was full of trays of artfully arranged culinary creations.

"Girls, this is Drew Montgomery, Caroline's friend from the *Dallas Journal of Business and Development*."

"Hi, Drew. I'm Pepper. We met at the wedding."

"Hello, I'm Sydney." He was surprised by her British accent. "I wasn't at the wedding, so I've never had the pleasure until now. It's lovely to see you."

Just then, Caroline entered the kitchen through a back door.

The mere sight of her kicked up his pulse. For the first time since he couldn't remember when, he wasn't sure if he should kiss her in front of her friends or keep a friendly, businesslike distance.

Since he was there in a professional capacity, he decided to keep it all business…at least until after the interview was over.

"Look who we have here, Caroline," Pepper said in a sing-song voice. "Isn't he just delicious?"

He laughed. *Delicious?* Okay, he'd never been called *delicious* in his entire life.

Caroline shot him an apologetic look but addressed her friend. "Pepper, really? You're embarrassing him. Look, you're making him blush."

He liked this lighter, more playful side of her.

"Whose side are you on?" he asked, joining in.

By that time she was standing next to him. "Well, your side, of course." She leaned in and planted a kiss on his lips, showing off for the girls, no doubt. It was slightly more than just a peck, lingering just long enough to make him want to lean in for more but not enough to make her friends suggest that they get a room. On the contrary. When they broke apart, Sydney whistled—an unexpected sound coming from someone with such a proper-sounding voice—a whistle that said, "Oh, Caroline, he is definitely a keeper."

Chapter Five

Tonight was the night.

Third date night.

The night that she could finally cast off the pretense of virtue, which for some reason had seemed so important when Caroline had gotten Drew to agree that if there was really going to be something between them that it couldn't be built on a foundation of sex. So they had restructured and restarted, reintroducing themselves so that they could get to know each other beyond the bedroom.

She had to give the guy a lot of credit for trying. For some reason, at the time they'd made the three-date agreement, it had seemed like a good idea. And really, it was, she reminded herself as she put on her lipstick, gave her hair one last tousle, wanting to look sexy, but not wanting to look like she had tried too hard.

Thank God, tonight was the night.

He'd suggested they go out to dinner, but instead, she had called him and said she had a recipe she wanted to try. That since their cake-baking date had gone so well last night—wait, last night *was* considered a date, wasn't it? He'd brought her dinner, they'd spent some good quality time together and while the kisses had been red-hot, that's where it had stopped. There had not been any discussion or debate about stopping or waiting for one more date.

Actually, this could be considered the fourth date, if you counted when he'd interviewed her and the girls for the *Journal* earlier that day. Okay, so it was all business and not so much pleasure— except for the kiss. She had seen him across the room, and something magnetic had pulled her to him.

She smiled to herself as she gave her bedroom one last once-over, making sure that everything was perfect for tonight. She had straightened her dressing table, putting away all of her makeup and creams and perfume. A strategically placed candle with an incidental book of matches lay in wait on the bureau. A brand-new box of condoms was tucked inside her nightstand. She would not be caught unprepared. No how, no way. Nothing would get in the way of the perfect ending to what would be their perfect night.

With one glance back at her four-poster bed, a white-hot jolt of longing coursed through her, warming her most personal places, places that longed for him. Tonight Drew would share her bed. It would be heaven waking up in his arms tomorrow.

Caroline made her way to the kitchen, where she set out the ingredients for her chicken marsala recipe. It was a simple dinner, and it wasn't that she was so terribly excited to try the recipe—in fact, her stomach was a little nervous from the anticipation of seeing him. Really, she had decided cooking for him was the way to go to give them extra time together.

It was already after eight-thirty. He said that once he finished at the paper it would probably be close to nine o'clock, and then he'd come over. He had to email this week's laid-out edition to the printer tonight before he left.

True to his word, Drew arrived shortly before

nine o'clock with a bottle of pinot noir to go with the chicken.

"Come on in," she said, leaning in and kissing him and then stepping back so he would follow her inside.

He smelled wonderful—notes of leather from that jacket he always wore, coffee and mint…it made her want to lean in and inhale the very essence of him.

She took his leather bomber jacket and hung it in the hall closet, then she pointed him in the direction of a corkscrew and two wineglasses she had set out for them. As he opened the bottle and she put the finishing touches on dinner, he talked about the Celebrations, Inc. article he'd written and had gotten off to the printer that night.

"I really think you're all going to be pleased when you see it," he said. "The photo came out great."

Simon, the photographer, had taken several different shots: a few solo photos of A.J. in the kitchen; some of her with the lovely spread of food she had put together specifically for the occasion; some mixed shots of A.J. with her friends.

For the most part, Caroline had done her best to stay out from in front of the camera until Simon and Drew had insisted on a group shot.

"Which picture did you choose?" Caroline asked, suddenly aware, for the first time, of all the excitement that had erupted over the opportunity to have a profile written about their new business endeavor. The exposure and positive PR it was sure to bring was phenomenal, but because of the article she might to need to explain to her father what she was doing moonlighting for a catering company.

"The group shot, of course. It's fabulous."

Oh, boy.

Her father knew that she had invested in A.J.'s business. Or at least she hoped he'd been paying attention on the occasions that she had mentioned she and Pepper had helped A.J. by investing seed money. Sydney had donated her expertise in marketing and PR, since she did not have the capital to invest. But Charles Coopersmith sometimes did not hear his own daughter when she talked to him about things other than Coopersmith & Bales business. He tended to have a one-track mind when it came to issues that did not directly involve him and the business that had been started by his grandfather.

Caroline had always written it off with the excuse that her father's one-track mind was what made him so successful. In fact, sometimes she wished her heart could be so doggedly dedicated to the family business. It sure would make life easier. She would be set financially—though of course she wouldn't have a life to speak of outside of the hallowed halls of Coopersmith & Bales, as evidenced by her father.

But Caroline had wanted more out of life. Not more money or more power. She wanted more of what was real—a husband, kids, the time and freedom to be there for her family rather than working seventy-hour weeks and being either so exhausted or preoccupied in the off hours that she was emotionally absent.

As she dished up the chicken, glancing at Drew as he poured wine into the goblets on the table, she thought, *I want more times like this, times like we had when we were baking last night.*

Her heart was close to overflowing. *Yes. This is exactly what I want.* The other thing she knew for sure was that she did not want to be the stand-in for the son her father never had. Her sister, Claudia, had been groomed to graduate from college with a token degree—something nonthreatening that would educate her, but their mother had raised her ultimately to be a wife and mother.

On the other hand, after it became apparent that he would not have a son, Charles Coopersmith had decided that Caroline, as his eldest daughter, would be the one to carry on the Coopersmith family legacy and step into his shoes once he retired. That fateful day was staring her down. The party was being planned. But she still had not formally given her father the word that she would take hold of the reins when he officially stepped down. He had been grooming her, and when she shared her ambivalence about accepting the promotion, he always reminded her that he'd pulled every string he could reach to ensure that Caroline had gotten into Harvard Business School. The way she could repay him was to make sure that the family legacy continued, to uphold the Coopersmith tradition of excellence in honor of all Coopersmiths past and those yet to come.

And now what did she want to do with her Harvard education? In the instant that she took the wineglass that Drew offered her and she clinked her glass to his, she knew. She wanted to bake cakes…and have Drew Montgomery's children.

As they ate dinner, she expressed her trepidations about being in the photo.

"I wish I would've asked you to run one of the shots without me in it. Or at least crop me out. Is it too late to recall the paper and crop me out?" she asked.

Drew simply laughed. "Sorry, the ink on the first hundred is probably already dry by now. Why are you so worried?"

She weighed her words. She was thirty-three years old and her father still dictated her life. It had been that way for so long—well, basically all her life—that she really did not think about it—except on the occasions when she brushed against the truth that she was going to have to make a decision about her future sooner than she wanted to admit. She couldn't see the absurdity of how she allowed her father to push her around until times like this…when she had to admit that she wasn't living the life she wanted to live.

"Well, you see," she said. "My father doesn't know that I actually work for Celebrations, Inc. He knows I've invested. Investing—as in being a silent partner—is one thing in his eyes. Actually baking and selling my baked goods is quite another."

Drew looked at her as if he were trying to understand. "So, is that why during the interview you stayed in the background? I noticed how you let your friends take the lead and tell me about the birth of Celebrations, Inc. and where they see it going."

Even though it was a little embarrassing to

admit that, yes, that was the reason, she said, "Well, yes, that and most of the time, I can't get a word in edgewise when we're all in the same room. But that's just the nature of our friendship. I don't feel slighted or otherwise compromised by their gregariousness."

She had loved the way Drew kept glancing at her during the interview, the way they exchanged knowing smiles as she had allowed her friends to dominate the conversation. It was as if she and Drew had their own telepathic dialogue going on, their own private conversation in the midst of her friends' excited retelling of stories and anecdotes.

"Why didn't you tell me before now?" he asked. "Even though the group shot was the best of the lot, you know I'd never do anything to purposely make you uncomfortable. Although, if you tell any of my journalistic colleagues that I gave you the option to dictate the direction of my article and photo, I'll be forced to deny it. My journalistic integrity would be at stake." He winked at her. "But seriously, why did you not say something before now?"

Why hadn't she? She shrugged. "I don't know. I guess I haven't completely decided where Celebrations, Inc. fits in my life beyond my investment. I mean, Coopersmith & Bales is… It's my family legacy. It's on my shoulders at least until one of Claudia's kids grows up and takes his place… or her place."

And Claudia's kids weren't even born yet. Basically, if she planned to pass the torch to one of Claudia's kids, she was sentencing herself to life at Coopersmith & Bales without a chance of parole, not until she was in her sixties at least. What did it say about her feelings if she was equating her life's work to a prison sentence?

"Maybe you didn't say anything because you want your father to know?" Drew suggested.

Yes…maybe…

"No…I just didn't think about the implications until now. Look, I don't want to talk about this tonight. I don't want to ruin a perfectly good dinner worrying about something that I can't solve overnight anyway."

It was true. While she did need to make a firm decision about her future at Coopersmith & Bales soon, there was no point in worrying about it now.

Drew stood up and took her by the hand and led her to the living room. For a second, she thought about steering him toward the bedroom, but she released the need for control just as fast as the idea had popped into her head.

Relax. Just go with it.

Since they'd agreed they would wait and get to know each other, Caroline had been imagining what it would be like to make love to him in her own bed. To spoon with him all night. To wake up in his arms the next morning.

Relax. Just go with it, she reminded herself. *Live in the moment. Right now.*

He put his arms around her and dusted her lips with kisses that trailed down her throat.

Forget the bedroom. She wanted him right there.

"Are you okay?" he asked, his lips still brushing hers ever so slightly.

"Oh, you have no idea how okay I am right now," she said, a little breathless.

He cradled her face in his palms and pressed his forehead to hers in that way that she had come to love. His sultry smile teased her, unleashing a need that had her longing to tell him exactly how many different ways she had imagined this moment—his kiss, his body, him in her bed. They no longer had to wait to enjoy each other.

But before the words could find their way past her lips, he led her to the couch, and his hands locked on her waist, as if he was taking possession of her body...and heart. She wanted to tell him he could have them. Both of them were already his, but she did not have to say it. He already seemed to understand.

She tucked herself into his chest, buried her face in his shirt, breathed in the scent of him— that delicious smell of cedar, coffee and leather. The scent that was so him that it hit her in a certain place that rendered her weak in the knees.

She breathed in deeply and melted into the heat of his body.

He smoothed a lock of hair off her forehead, kissed the skin he'd just uncovered and searched her eyes. She answered him with a kiss that said, *Yes, I want this. I want you,* as she savored the warmth of him, the scent of his skin that clung to him the same way she wanted to cling to him because she wanted them to be *that* close.

He kissed her softly, gently, until her fingers found their way into his thick, dark hair, pulling him close, closer—until they were kissing with a need so furious it was all-consuming.

The next thing she knew, his hands had found hers, and he laced their fingers together. She looked at his hands entwined in hers. They were big and handsome—masculine hands. They lingered a moment, gripping, flexing, hesitating, as if he were silently giving her one last chance to change her mind, to flee, to back out of what was about to happen.

But no, she wanted it to happen.

My God, it's finally going to happen... Oh, how I've missed this.

A rush of red-hot need spiraled through her. He must have read it in her face, because he let go of her hands and his arms closed around her. In a fevered rush, he claimed her mouth, her mind, her reason.

Her fingers slipped into his curly dark hair again and held him close as her lips parted on a sigh and gave him full permission to take possession of every inch of her, as she clung to him, relishing the closeness. There was no mistaking his need, his desire. She could feel it grow as his hands swept down the outer edge of her body to claim her derriere.

Then somehow, in a heated whirlwind of passion, his hands slid underneath her sweater, finding bare skin. The contact of skin on skin made her breathe in sharply.

A warm palm slipped under her bra and splayed over one of her breasts. His fingers moved from one nipple to the other and then trailed down her belly, where they lingered and played, tracing small circles that made her stomach muscles tighten and spasm in agonizing pleasure. Then his hand slid even farther still, teasing its way down to the edge of her skirt's waistband, toward a silken, hidden place that had been begging for his touch. But all he did was trace the edge of her waistband.

She tried to live in the moment, focusing only on that second…but the way she needed him was driving her to the brink of insanity, especially the way he was kissing her neck.

Driven by passion, her fingers swept over his tight shoulders and muscled arms, exploring the firm sinew before going south and discovering the curve of his derriere. She pulled him even closer so that the hardness of him pressed into her, urging her legs to part, proving to her that his need was as strong as hers.

He claimed her mouth again, capturing her tongue, teasing her until she almost couldn't bear it any longer. But with every fiber of her being she concentrated on the moment, until she thought she would burst with longing.

Finally, she tried to maneuver her hands to the button of his jeans, needing to push them away and get rid of the barriers between them so that they stood naked and wanting. Together.

As unselfconscious as they were that first night together.

But he stopped her, holding her so close that she could hear his heart beat.

"I have to go now." His voice sounded hoarse and raspy.

He was leaving? For a moment, she thought she had heard him wrong. But when she looked up at him, she read in his eyes that she had, indeed, heard him correctly. But, through the haze of her need, she saw him smiling down at her. His lips were swollen and red, and she desperately want to taste them again.

But he wanted to leave?

Now?

"What? Drew, why?" she asked, doubt suddenly flooding her senses. "What's wrong?"

"Not a single thing is wrong," he said. "I want you in the worst way. It's taking every ounce of strength I have to keep from making love to you right now. But I know how important it is to you to believe that what we have is even more powerful than the want and need I'm feeling for you right now." He closed his eyes and clenched his fists, inhaling then exhaling a deep breath before he looked at her again. "But the next time I see you…" His sultry smile made her want to take him right there. *To hell with next time.*

"Next time," he nodded. "Between now and then, I want you to think about how good it's going to be next time. I intend to wake up with you in my arms."

He pulled her into his arms and kissed her, proving he meant every word he said. He held her until she had digested everything he'd said, until her heart dismantled the wall of self-protection that she had been quickly building since she'd met him and convinced herself that he was just another guy who was passing through his life, on his way somewhere, too busy to make a permanent commitment. But the way he held her silenced the loud voice of doubt that babbled on in her head suggesting that he was rejecting her—

But he wasn't. Even though she had built up this third date in her head to be something grand and passionate, really what she wanted, what she needed, was *this*—the closeness they were sharing right now.

As his lips found hers again and brushed them with a whisper-soft kiss, she tore down the rest of the wall.

Okay. So, we aren't going to make love. Not yet. But they'd waited this long. She could wait a little longer. Because he was worth it. And because here in his arms, she felt safe and powerful…like she could actually have the life she really wanted.

Chapter Six

Despite a rather restless night, Caroline was in the office by eight o'clock the next morning. She had just sat down at her desk with a cup of coffee when her cell phone rang. It was Sydney bubbling over with excitement.

"Did you see it?" she asked. "It's fabulous. The article is absolutely fabulous. He did such a great job. You are one lucky woman."

"I am a lucky woman," Caroline said, although she was still doing battle with the destructive doubt demons that danced with her thoughts, trying to seduce her into believing Drew had left last night because his interest had waned. They were having lunch today. Everything was okay. She couldn't allow herself to think otherwise. "But I haven't had a chance to get my hands on a copy yet because I just sat down at my desk."

"Okay," Sydney continued. "When you check your email, you'll have an email from me with a press release I wrote about the article this morning. It has a link to the story. I sent it out to our contact list."

Caroline turned on her computer. "My gosh, you've done all this and it's not even eight-thirty? Do you ever sleep?"

"Not last night, hon," she said. "I was too excited about this opportunity."

That was precisely the reason that Sydney was so good at what she did.

"How are things at work?" she asked.

Sydney let out a quiet moan. "Tense as ever." She lowered her voice to a whisper. "The latest rumor predicts mass layoffs as early as next week, but that was the word last month and nothing happened. It's beginning to feel like those end-of-the-world predictions that get everyone all stirred up and they never happen."

Caroline chuckled and opened the email that Sydney had sent her.

"I'm just trying to keep my head down, do my work and stay out of everyone's way."

"Sounds like a good plan," Caroline said as she opened the file containing Sydney's press release. It had been sent from the Celebrations, Inc. account. Sydney must have been working on this in the wee hours of the morning. No doubt with her trepidations, she wouldn't chance sending it through the Texas Star server—even if she did only sign on to access the Celebrations, Inc. account. She was much too business savvy to take a chance like that.

"Say, I was wondering if you could please ask Drew if he could grant us permission to copy the article so we can use it in our press kit and customer literature?"

"Sure," Caroline said. "I'm seeing him for lunch today. I'll ask him then. By the way, great press release, Syd."

"Thanks, love," she said. "I'd better run. I won't be doing myself any favors if I get caught on a personal call. Another rumor has it that the phone lines are tapped."

They both laughed at the absurdity of the suggestion. Caroline was glad to see that Sydney seemed better able to put things into perspective. She did not blame her for worrying, however. Her livelihood was at stake. Sydney did not have the benefit of falling back on a trust fund or family money. She was completely on her own. That was one of the many reasons Caroline respected her so much. As they hung up, Caroline made a mental note to let Sydney know the next time a marketing or public relations position opened at Coopersmith & Bales. Not that she wanted to steal her friend away—Texas Star was one of C & B's biggest clients—but at least at a place like C & B, there wasn't the constant talk about the sky falling. But then again, at the rate Celebrations, Inc. was gaining traction, pretty soon A.J. might be able to pay Sydney enough to come on board full-time at the catering company.

After they hung up, Caroline clicked on the link to the story that Sydney had provided in the press release. The browser opened, revealing a full-color photo of the group of four friends gathered around the food display that A.J. had created. Drew was right. It was a great photo of all of them. Definitely one for the scrapbook, possibly a good publicity shot if the *Journal's* policies allowed businesses to purchase the rights to their photos.

The story, which couldn't have been more complimentary if Sydney had written it herself, was on the third page. Caroline wondered if there was even the slightest chance that her father might overlook it.

Ha! The chance was slim to none. He did not get to the rank he held in the business world by overlooking the details—especially a profile of a new business that would definitely need the services of an accounting firm to offer financial and tax guidance. And if, per chance, Charles Coopersmith had missed it, someone on staff was bound to bring it to his attention.

He pretty much had all the bases covered.

Caroline glanced at the Waterford crystal clock on the mahogany credenza behind her desk. It was eight-twenty.

Caroline braced herself for the inevitable.

Let's see how long it takes him to say something about the article.

An hour later her cell phone rang again. This time it was A.J.

Caroline expected to have a celebratory talk with A.J. similar to the one she had with Sydney, but once they got past the initial excitement, A.J. revealed that there was, in fact, another reason for her call.

"I don't know how in the world I'm going to repay Drew for the recognition the *Journal* profile has already generated. You won't believe this, but I received an interesting business proposal this morning."

"What do you mean?"

Caroline looked up to see a scowling Margaret Daily, a Coopersmith & Bales tax accountant, paused in the doorway of her office.

"Hold on just a moment, A.J." Caroline held her cell phone away from her ear. "Margaret, may I help you with something?"

Margaret was one of the younger C & B employees. Caroline guessed they were about the same age, but everything about Margaret seemed older. Much older. Especially the frown and furrowed brow that seemed to be the woman's permanent expression.

This morning, as she lurked in the threshold of Caroline's office, the woman was not only scowling but she looked like she smelled something particularly foul.

As she stepped into the office, Caroline noticed she was holding a copy of the *Dallas Journal of Business and Development.*

Uh-oh. A knot formed in the pit of Caroline's stomach and cinched tighter when Margaret held up the paper opened to page 3.

Margaret—with her brown frizzy hair, makeup-free face and navy business suit that was half a size too small—stabbed at the article with her index finger. "Is this *you?*" There was such disdain in her voice that Caroline bristled.

"Apparently so, Margaret. Isn't that what the caption says?"

She knew she shouldn't let the nasty woman get to her, but who did she think she was barging in her office with an attitude, obviously spoiling for a fight? Caroline had always gone out of her way to be civil to the woman because she could tell Margaret was of the attitude that *she* had scrapped for everything she had, whereas Caroline had been installed in the office via the route of the silver spoon.

"It must be nice to have time to bake cakes, when it's all I can do to get my job here at C & B done. Isn't it against company policy to moonlight?"

Moonlight? Is she kidding? Who even uses words like that?

Suddenly, Caroline was tired of apologizing for her circumstances. So many times, she had stepped back and let Margaret's passive-aggressive remarks roll right over her because she did not want to be the office bitch, the boss's daughter, the sacred one who had her way paved because she happened to have the right daddy.

"Margaret, perhaps if you spent more time focusing on your job and less time worrying about things that don't concern you, you might have time to bake a cake every once in a while."

Caroline did not want to be nasty. Really, she had tried to stop herself, but enough was enough. As Margaret stood there spewing her derision, Caroline saw her life flash in front of her eyes. This miserable woman standing before her was her coworker, her peer. Caroline had absolutely nothing in common with her, yet each day she stayed being miserable, mentally preparing herself to take over for her father when he retired. A life sentence of doing a job she did not want to do was one step closer to becoming as miserable as Margaret Daily. Not that one had to socialize with her coworkers, but this woman seemed to embody everything Caroline hated about C & B, about the world of accounting, about where her future was heading…and fast.

Margaret continued to stare at her with an unchanged, hateful expression, but she did not say anything. Oh, but she did not have to. Caroline could virtually read her thoughts. And they weren't pretty.

"May I help you with anything else, Margaret? Perhaps something work related?"

The wretched woman rolled her eyes, turned on her heel and left without saying another word.

Caroline blinked at the place where the stink of Margaret's bad attitude seemed to linger like a dark cloud. Talk about a chip on her shoulder.

"Are you still there?" she said into the phone.

"Yes, I am. Uhh…wow. Who was that?"

"One of my fabulous coworkers. So, obviously you heard the exchange."

"I did, I'm sorry to say." A.J. cleared her throat. "Well, maybe what I have to tell you will cheer you up. And your encounter with Miss Merry Sunshine will give you the impetus to come. Even if you have plans."

Caroline sat back in her leather office chair and switched the cell phone to her other ear, making herself comfortable. "Right, the interesting business proposal you mentioned before we were so rudely interrupted. What's going on?"

"So, I get a phone call this morning—no. I'm not going to tell you over the phone. Just come by the office tonight. Seven o'clock. Believe me, you'll think it's worth it. I'm going to call Pepper and Sydney, too. We all need to be there."

"I have plans with Drew tonight," she said.

"Even better. Bring Superman—or should I

Send For
2 FREE BOOKS
Today!

I accept your offer!

Please send me two free
Harlequin® Special Edition
novels and two mystery gifts
(gifts worth about $10).
I understand that these books
are completely free—even
the shipping and handling will
be paid—and I am under no
obligation to purchase anything, ever,
as explained on the back of this card.

235/335 HDL FNP4

Please Print

FIRST NAME

LAST NAME

ADDRESS

APT.#   CITY

STATE/PROV.   ZIP/POSTAL CODE

Visit us online at
www.ReaderService.com

call him Clark Kent, since he might find another story in this?"

"What are you talking about, A.J.?"

"It's a *business* surprise, and that's all I'm going to say. I know it sounds crazy and it's totally last minute, but it's important that all of us are here."

Silence stretched across the line. Caroline moved her computer mouse and the screen saver disappeared, revealing the webpage boasting the Celebrations, Inc. story. She stared at the smiling faces of her friends and thought about what a breath of fresh air they were compared to grumpy Margaret Daily.

"Look, just please trust me," A.J. pleaded. "I wouldn't ask this of you under most other circumstances. But I'll tell you something in confidence…just promise that you won't say anything to Pepper and Sydney. Please don't tell them, okay? I want them to be surprised."

"Okay."

"Tomorrow, two very interesting, rather prominent people will be joining us to present this business proposition. And the offer involves all four of us."

"Really?" she asked as she called up a file she

needed to work on after she got off the phone with
A.J. "Who is it?"

"I've already told you too much. Just come tonight and bring Drew. I promise it will be worth
your while."

Hmm... In her mind, she saw Drew's earnest
expression as he promised that he would definitely
make their next night together worth the wait.

However, surely this business surprise of A.J.'s
wouldn't last all night. Since Caroline had dis-
pensed business advice to Celebrations, Inc. as
well as serving as her part-time pastry chef, she
figured A.J. wanted her there to judge whether it
was a sound opportunity. Caroline's curiosity was
definitely piqued.

"As long as you're not trying to rope us into
one of those multilevel marketing schemes, I suppose we can rearrange our plans to stop by," Caroline said.

"Thank you! Come hungry, because I'll have
lots of food."

"I would be disappointed if you didn't have a
spread. But are you sure you won't give me any
more hints as to what this is all about?"

"Tonight. You'll see that I've already told you
too much. And remember, act like you don't know
a thing, okay? Pepper and Sydney would never

forgive me for telling you more than I told them. Then again, after they hear the news, I'd wager that they wouldn't be upset for long. See you tonight."

Caroline hung up the phone and glanced up to see her father standing in the same place Margaret had occupied earlier. The look on his face made Margaret's expression look angelic.

When Drew walked into the office, Bia was waiting for him with a stack of Texas Star quarterly earnings statements in one hand and a notebook in the other.

"I have to talk to you right away," she said.

"Good morning to you, too, Beatrice. May I please have a cup of coffee first?"

"I put a fresh, hot cup on your desk one minute before you walked in." She followed him into his office and shut the door before he could object.

Sure enough, there was not one but two cups of steaming coffee and a box of doughnut holes on his desk.

"I brought you doughnuts," she said. "You have to make time for me."

He plucked one from the open box and popped it into his mouth, washing it down with a swallow of coffee that was still a tad too hot.

He grimaced.

"Plus," she said. "I have some pretty exciting news that I really think you're going to be happy to hear."

His gaze shot to the Texas Star reports and then back to Bia. He knew what she was going to say before she said it. Suddenly, the doughnut felt like a leaden weight in his gut.

"You've cracked the story?" he asked.

"Welll…" she drawled. "Let's just say, I've discovered a minor chink in the Texas Star armor."

He took another draw of his coffee. Somehow the heat did not burn him this time—probably because the possibility of a break in this story turning into something big could spell rough times for him and Caroline. Because Texas Star was one of C & B's biggest clients and because Pepper was her best friend. But if there was a story there it was his duty to report it.

But *story* was the operative word. He wasn't into publishing half-baked stories or something-out-of-nothing stories. Nope, it would have to be valid, something they could substantiate. That's what Bia had to show him right now.

He breathed in deeply and blew out his breath. "Okay, B, lay it on me."

She studied him for a minute, and the way her

gaze bore into him, it almost felt as though she were reading him.

"I know this might cause a problem for you and your girlfriend." She paused, as if giving him time to answer. He chose not to say anything. He knew Bia was perceptive, but some things were private.

"I know the guidelines of when I should recuse myself. Whatcha got?"

Bia quirked a brow at him, a nonverbal message that said she was seeing through his bravado. She opened her notebook.

"See this?" She pointed to two columns. "Look at how the debt-to-capital ratio increased by forty percent over the past year. The stock is selling for almost one hundred dollars a share. That's an eighty percent increase over the past year. Yet they have gigantic debt. So if this company is so astoundingly profitable, why do they keep accruing debt? There's a story here. I just need to keep digging."

Drew picked up her notebook and squinted at the figures on the page. Crap, she was right. Something wasn't adding up. Damn it.

He set down the notebook and rubbed his eyes. He knew what he had to do. If Caroline was not in his life, he would be all over this story. He'd make sure a reporter was living on the Texas Star doorstep…and if that didn't work, he himself would be tempted to camp out on Harris Merriweather's portico.

As hard as it was to admit it to himself, after the above bases had been covered, one of the first doors he'd be knocking on for answers to his questions was Texas Star's auditor—Coopersmith & Bales.

Chapter Seven

Judging by the look on her father's face, Caroline knew the best thing she could do was to invite him into her office and close the door.

"Hi, Dad. Please come in."

She tried to make her voice sound pleasant—not too cheery, but certainly not timid, as if she were admitting she had done something wrong. Despite the assertion that Margaret had made, she was not violating a moonlighting clause. She was free to have another job as long as it did not interfere with her work at the firm. She was relieved that her voice did not shake and that her father did do just as she had hoped. He came in and shut the door behind him.

That's when she noticed the rolled-up copy of the *Dallas Journal of Business and Development* gripped in his left hand. He had been holding it behind his back as he stood in the doorway.

Caroline wondered if it was the same copy Margaret had been brandishing. Then again, their office received multiple copies—one for each department. It seemed everyone had seen an actual paper copy but her. Thank goodness she had had time to look it up online to see the picture of herself and her friends…er, *business partners*. Imagine that—working somewhere that you actually liked and respected your colleagues, and in turn, they liked and respected you.

Her father stood in front of her desk, hulking over her. He was a tall, imposing man with dark hair that had gone distinguished gray at the temples. She had gotten his green eyes, but right now, his were the color of a stormy sea.

Despite his intimidating posture, Caroline was bound and determined to let him speak first, adhering to her first rule of business: he who speaks first loses.

Charles Coopersmith stood staring at her for

a long half a minute—which was a long, uncomfortable time in a faceoff.

Finally, he said, "Please explain this."

He tossed the paper onto her desk with a quick flick of his wrist, as if he were skimming a stone on a glassy lake. It slid across the polished wood surface and landed in front of her, upside down.

She reached out and turned it so that the article faced her the right way. Holding on to the edges, she said a silent prayer that he couldn't see that her hands were shaking.

"Ahh, yes, this." She manufactured her best smile as she gazed at the article. "It's the catering company that my friend A. J. Sherwood-Antonelli started. Pepper Merriweather invested in it, too. We were fortunate to get some rather nice press. It will be good for business."

"When did you get involved in this business venture? Why did not you bother asking me before you went off half-cocked and made an investment?"

His words stung on so many levels. Did the man not ever hear a word she said to him? Did he have that little respect for her? If he thought her so incompetent, why was he so hell-bent on her stepping into his shoes when he retired in a few short weeks?

"I did tell you. Numerous times."

"No, you did not. Because I wouldn't have allowed such a foolish investment. A catering company? Really, Caroline? Investments in the food industry are notoriously risky. I hope you didn't fork over a lot of money."

So, it was the cash investment, not the fact that she was baking on the side, that rankled him? A sarcastic retort about his selective hearing was on the tip of her tongue, but she checked herself. She needed to be careful to sound confident but not flippant.

"Well, yes. To be clear, Dad, I'll bet I brought up Celebrations, Inc. at least a half dozen times. But whenever I try to talk to you about something other than Coopersmith & Bales, you never seem to hear me. This is case in point."

He furrowed his brow and looked a little confused, but only for a moment. Then he waved away her comment and his gruff stance was back in place.

"I'm too busy for that kind of foolishness." He leaned forward and slapped his hand down on the newspaper. "Why the hell does the article list you as the pastry chef for this Celebrations, Inc.?"

Okay. Here we go.

She looked at him, locking gazes, reminding

herself that she had not done anything wrong. Nothing except let him intimidate and bully her into investing the best part of herself in something she hated doing.

"Because *I am* the pastry chef for Celebrations, Inc. If you took an interest, maybe you wouldn't have to learn about things like this in the paper."

He flinched, as if her back talk surprised him. Really, his shock shouldn't surprise her, because in the past, she had never had anything in her life worth challenging him over. Before this. She meant no disrespect—he was her father, after all—but it was time *she* started commanding respect from *him*.

"You do realize when you are promoted to senior partner, you won't have time to dabble in foolishness like this any longer."

Foolishness? He really was clueless, wasn't he? He had no idea who she was or what made her happy. If she asked him right now, he most certainly wouldn't have an inkling about what mattered to her in life. What she was passionate about.

It suddenly struck her that he probably did not even realize the author of the article had been the best man in his own daughter's wedding. How could a man be so good at what he did yet so oblivious in all the other facets of his life that should matter?

If that was what it took to be an effective senior partner, then she definitely wasn't the woman for the job. Even if it meant that this generation of Coopersmiths would not be represented in the upper echelon at the firm.

"You really don't know me, do you?" The words escaped before she could rein them in.

"What?" he spat, obviously surprised by her insubordination.

"I said you don't know me very well, because if you did you would realize that I would rather bake than bank. You'd also realize that despite what you want, I am not the best person to step into your shoes after you retire. I'm not you, and honestly, Dad, it breaks my heart to admit it, but I don't want to be like you. So, this is as good a time as any to let you know that I won't be accepting the senior partner position when you retire."

This time he looked like the one who had been slapped. After a few beats of astonished silence, he changed his tone.

"Caroline, let's not make hasty declarations here. If you feel as if I haven't spent enough time with you and you're not adequately prepared for the job, we can work on that."

She shook her head. He *really* did not get it, did he?

"No, Dad, you don't understand—"

He held up a hand, fending off her words. "Richard is counting on you to come on board. We've already have everything laid out. The plan is set."

"No, I'm not—"

"Shhh!" He held out his hand like a mad traffic cop.

He'd shushed her?

"This," she said, gesturing at him. "This is exactly what I mean when I say that you don't hear me when I talk to you. I'm not accepting the promotion, Dad. You and Richard will need to make other arrangements. If you don't want to tell him, I will."

Charles Coopersmith insisted that Caroline take the rest of the day off to think about things. At first, that was the last thing she wanted to do—especially since the day off was mandated by her father and the entire office would probably put two and two together and believe that she had been sent home as a reprimand for the *Journal* article.

After she thought about it for a while, sitting

at her desk, unproductively churning the conversation with her father around in her head for the better part of an hour, she decided to leave and do something more productive. Something that would make her happy.

At first she thought about baking a chocolate pie using rich seventy percent cocoa that had been imported from Belgium, but then she realized there was only one thing that would satisfy her appetite right now.

She called Drew and asked him to meet her at her condo for…lunch.

When he got there and she answered the door wearing the hideous pumpkin-colored bridesmaid dress that had seemed to work its magic the night of the wedding, he just stood there in the threshold, looking at her like she was something on the dessert cart at Manuel's and he was starving. At least she hoped that's what his intense, brooding expression meant.

She did not give him a chance to prove her wrong or explain it away. She wrapped herself around him, kissing him hard on the mouth, all lips and tongue and "take me right now" touches.

She wanted to lose herself in him, show him how much she had been aching for him. She wanted to show him with her lips and hands and body how much she had missed the physical pull of their relationship. And while his declaration last night—about how he wanted to prove to her that she meant more to him than the red-hot love they made—was sweet, she certainly wasn't going to let one more day go by with them denying that part of their relationship.

They'd proven that they were all that and so much more.

So as she kissed him right there in the foyer, he responded, holding her and touching her and tasting her back. She felt his body respond as he swelled and hardened. She loved the feel of how her curves fit so well with the hard angles of his body. When he moved his hands to her hips, claiming her body and pulling her closer, she arched against him, plumbing the depth of his desire.

"I've missed this so much," she murmured breathlessly. "Please tell me you're not going to stop us this time...."

He raised his finger to her lips, then he covered her mouth with his, silencing her and answering her question all at once.

His hands were on her breasts, cupping them through the pumpkin satin, teasing her hard nipples. She gasped. Her head fell back and she closed her eyes, losing herself in his touch.

It felt so damn good to be in his arms again, knowing where this was going, knowing that they were so worth the wait.

She slid her hand down the front of his trousers and claimed his erection, teasing him over and over, rubbing and stroking his desire through the layers of his pants.

When he picked her up and carried her over to the couch, kissing her throat and playfully biting down on her earlobe, it was almost more than she could stand.

The thought of making love to him right there in the living room sent a hungry shudder racking her whole body. Suddenly she needed him naked and on top of her so that he could bury himself inside of her.

Now. Right now.

As if reading her mind, he unzipped her dress. She shrugged out of it, letting it fall to the floor, leaving her wearing only the high heels and thigh-high stockings—the only undergarment that she had put on under the dress.

He inhaled sharply at the sight of her standing there and held her away from him for a moment so that he could look at her reverently for a moment.

She reached out and unbuttoned his pants and slid down the zipper, and he moved to free himself of the clothes.

It felt like the first time again—no, better than the first time, because she knew him so well now. She knew that she loved him and wanted to savor this moment of reunion.

At the rate he was going, if he didn't slow down, it would be over before he showed her just how much he loved her. So he slowed down, kissing her neck as she undid each button on his blue oxford shirt. When she was done, he shrugged it aside so that it dropped to the floor. In one swift, gentle motion they stood there naked together.

He had not set out with the intention of making love to her. When she had called, he'd been so conflicted about what to say to her—whether to tell her about Bia's article or to wait. Because the implications posed such a threat to them, he just needed to see her, to try and make some sense of what he should do, how he should handle it with her. And then she answered the door wearing that dress—that ridiculously sexy pumpkin-colored dress—and all reason went out of his mind.

He knew exactly what that dress meant and what she wanted, and damn it, he wanted her, too.

She stood there in front of him in only her stockings and heels, looking sweeter and much more tempting than anything he'd ever seen in his life. How in the world had he been able to resist her?

Well, the only reason was that he'd wanted to prove to her that she meant more to him than the incredibly powerful physical draw they had on one another.

This chemical reaction was an important part of who they were together, but it was a bonus. Since it had meant so much to Caroline to prove that there was more, he was absolutely willing to do whatever it took to make her happy.

He cupped her breasts in his hands and then lowered his head to them. In turn, he took each one into his mouth, suckling them until she cried out. The sound of her pleasure aroused him even more.

Despite the need that was driving him to the edge of insanity, once again, he purposely slowed down, taking a moment to savor how beautiful she looked and to bask in how much he loved her.

He wanted to tell her he would never, ever hurt her. Not on purpose. Never on purpose. As they lay together naked, body to body, skin to skin, she reached for him and kissed him deeply. All at once it was as if someone had turned up the heat. The two of them were all tongues thrusting, hands exploring, teeth nipping—hungrily devouring each other. Until he was sure she was ready for him. Then he buried himself inside her, knowing without a doubt that right here, right now, making love to her was where he needed to be. Because the more he knew about Caroline, the more he realized his life was nothing without her.

Caroline's call had been unexpected. After they made love, he'd stayed with her the rest of the afternoon, calling Bia, asking her to handle things while he dealt with some personal things.

Caroline had told him it had been a hectic morning of back-to-back meetings, most of which had run overtime. She had said something about a run-in with her father that she had to tell him about later. She said she did not want to cloud their afternoon. It was clear that she wasn't herself. So he'd held her as they both dozed on and off, waking to make love again until the sun had set and it was time for them to shower and meet her friends.

He'd pondered what to do with the news Bia had delivered about the crack in the Texas Star case. Since Bia had enough of a lead to work with to pursue an investigative story, Drew had no choice but to recuse himself from the project. His relationship with Caroline muddied the waters and made it a conflict of interest for him to even act as the editor of the project. Making love to Caroline made the muddy waters even murkier.

That meant Bia had to handle the investigation and the editing of any resulting pieces on her own. She had been so giddy that she had done a happy dance right in his office, after which she had promptly apologized for the awkward position in which her good fortune had put Drew.

While he could fully understand his protégée's exuberance—stories such as this did not present themselves every day, and she was proving herself to have the instincts of a top-rate journalist—this story could have the potential to destroy Drew's personal life.

He was in love with Caroline. It was as plain and simple as that. And if this piece panned out the way his gut was telling him it would, well... plain and simple, it spelled disaster, despite the fact that he had removed himself.

He took a deep breath and reminded himself that Bia had yet to talk to the folks at Coopersmith & Bales. Before that happened, Drew needed to decide if he would forewarn Caroline, which could put her in a bad position. But then again, if

Coopersmith & Bales, one of the nation's oldest accounting firms, was as clean as he hoped, there wouldn't be a problem.

Not that he suspected Caroline of dirty accounting, he reinforced for probably the hundredth time that day. In fact, that she had brought up the unrest at Texas Star that night of their first date made him believe she knew very little—if anything at all—about the inner workings of the C & B/Texas Star relationship.

Drew and Caroline parked on the street in front of the Celebrations, Inc. Catering Company office at seven sharp.

Still, judging by the cars parked on the street and in the small lot, everyone else was already here.

Drew walked around and opened Caroline's door, offering a hand to help her out of the car. They'd both been quiet on the drive over. As a pang of unease flooded through him, he reminded himself, yet again, that it was still too early to tell Caroline about the Texas Star investigation.

Because if the story panned out to be a big nothing, there was no use in upsetting her.

That was the right thing to do.

Wasn't it?

Chapter Eight

Drew took Caroline's hand as they walked up the driveway and around back to Celebrations, Inc.'s kitchen door. That was one of the little things she loved about their relationship—the way it was so natural for them to hold hands, as if it were a way to stay connected.

Since they did not see any signs of life in the front of the house—beyond the display in the shop's plate-glass windows—she figured this surprise business proposition was happening around back.

"Any clue what this is about?" Drew asked. "I mean, am I here as a friend or reporter?"

He shot her a smile that warmed her heart.

"I have no clue," she said. "I'm just glad you're here."

He leaned in and planted a kiss on her cheek. The feel of him so near washed away the residual yuck that had colored her day.

With Drew holding her hand and the big surprise, things would stay on the upward grade. Judging by A.J.'s insistence on gathering everyone, it had to be something real. A.J. was not a drama queen. Now, Pepper would have no qualms about calling an emergency meeting to help her pick out a pair of shoes; Sydney might call a meeting—or more like an intervention—asking her friends to *stop* her from buying a pair of shoes. But A.J. was nearly as steady and steadfast as Caroline herself.

When A.J. said something was important, it was bound to be important. And though Caroline did not understand why everything had to be so intriguingly clandestine, the big surprise had provided a welcome thought diversion after the face-off with her father.

True to form, he refused to hear what she was saying and insisted on her taking some time to think it over before informing the other senior partner, Richard Bales, that she was abdicating.

Even though her father had refused to accept the fact that Caroline had no interest in abandoning her work with Celebrations, Inc. to sell her soul to the family business, the time-out had given her perspective to see that she really shouldn't abandon her position at C & B altogether. Celebrations, Inc. was poised on the brink of bigger things, but it might put too much financial strain on the company to expect to draw a salary. She was levelheaded enough to know that she had bills to pay, and since she had tapped into the maximum that she was allowed to draw from her trust fund, she needed the steady income that her position at C & B provided.

That didn't mean she had to accept the senior partner position, though.

"Here we go." Caroline pointed toward a nondescript door on the side of the building.

"You know you're part of the family when you get to enter through the friends-and-family door," she said.

"Friends and family, huh? It's not the door for the hired help?"

She loved his sense of humor, how being around him made her feel better, lighter, *passionate*. The chimes tinkled as she pulled the door open. She had to smile to herself, because before A.J. met her fiancé, her good friend had been just this side of paranoid about safety. She had kept the place locked up tighter than a Fort Knox vault.

Wasn't it wonderful how a little love and security could change a person's entire outlook on life?

When Caroline entered the kitchen, she saw her three friends, along with A.J.'s fiancé, Shane Harrison, as well as a handsome man and blond woman, both of whom looked vaguely familiar, but she couldn't pinpoint how she knew them.

Everyone sat on stools around the huge granite-topped island digging into a gorgeous spread— even more elaborate than the one she had set up for Drew when he'd interviewed them. A.J. must have worked on it all day. The way it was displayed looked like it might have been set up to tempt an important potential client or for another, more elaborate photo shoot as a good example of the kind of magic A.J. could work with food. Judging by the way the crowd was feasting, Caroline figured it must have been the former.

A.J. was the first to notice her. "Caroline and Drew, I'm so glad you're here."

Every head turned and all eyes were on her. She smiled and waved a greeting. "Sorry I'm late."

"Nonsense," said A.J. "You're not late. You're right on time. Come in and grab a plate—there are places for you right over here—but first, I'd like for you to meet Carlos Montigo and Lindsay Bingham-Montigo. You might know them from their Epicurean Traveler Network show, *The Diva Drives*. And of course, before that, Lindsay hosted *The Diva Dishes*."

Oh! Well, of course. That's why they looked familiar. Caroline adored food TV—almost as much as she adored baking—and had probably seen every episode of the short-lived food and travel show that had Carlos and Lindsay driving all over Europe showcasing fascinating places and regional food. They'd had a great on-air chemistry, and they'd ended up falling in love and getting married.

She glanced at Drew. Of course he would be the first person to pop into her mind, as he often did these days when the words *chemistry* and *falling in love* were mentioned. Actually, it was more apt to say that when he wasn't with her, he'd taken up residence in the far recesses of her mind… and heart.

She was so glad he'd been amenable to switching their plans to come here tonight.

Carlos and Lindsay were standing now and

offering outstretched hands. Caroline and Drew both stepped forward and shook their proffered hands. Yes, now that she could put them into context, she absolutely recognized them.

For a split second, she was a little starstruck, or maybe it was just the sheer beauty of both of them that got to her. Whatever it was, Caroline felt a little silly. That alone helped her find her voice and pull herself together.

"So nice to meet you."

"You, too," said Lindsay. "Please, come join us. A.J. said you rearranged your plans to see us tonight."

Caroline realized she had been wondering if having dinner with them was A.J.'s big surprise, but then she distinctly remembered her saying "business proposal." She was almost too curious to eat.

Even so, she and Drew made their way around to their seats at the other side of the kitchen island. She fixed herself a modest plate of fruit, curried chicken salad and asparagus frittata that had been topped with crème fraiche and chives. A.J. had outdone herself. But Caroline couldn't help but notice the conspicuous absence of sweets. The realization brought mixed emotions—on one hand, at least A.J. had not asked her to start baking this afternoon.

But that meant there was no dessert!

After Caroline and Drew were settled into their places at the island, A.J. said, "On behalf of Carlos and Lindsay, thank you for coming on such short notice. I hope you'll be as excited as I am once you know why we've gathered everyone tonight. I'll turn things over to Carlos and Lindsay to tell you more."

Carlos set down his fork and wiped his mouth with his napkin.

"I'm glad you all know our television work. Did you also know that we took a brief hiatus to open a restaurant in North Carolina that helps at-risk youth find an identity and safe path via the food industry? Now that the restaurant is thriving, Lindsay and I are up for a new challenge. We would like to produce a reality television show for Epicurean Traveler. We'd like to follow a catering company, and you were referred to us by Princess Sophie of St. Michel. She is friends with your friend Margeaux Broussard, who assured us you were the only catering company for the job." He winked, and Caroline could see just how charming he was. "Plus, it must have been kismet, because we saw the fabulous profile of you and your establishment in the newspaper. We are only here for a few days, but if you are agreeable, we'd like to talk to you tonight about the concept for the show."

How wonderful for A.J.!

"No disrespect to my lovely wife," Carlos continued. "But I can see why Margeaux would recommend you. You are lovely women, each and every one of you. If you're in agreement, we'd like to schedule a time in the next two days to do some test shots to aid us in our casting decision."

What? Caroline and Drew looked at each other.

Pepper squealed. Sydney sat there looking stunned.

Caroline's head swam with questions. Was he really suggesting that she, A.J., Pepper and Sydney take part in his new reality show?

Of course, Pepper managed to gush exactly what Caroline was thinking. "So, you're saying you might want us to star in your new series?"

Carols and Lindsay looked at each other and grinned.

"That's what we'd like to discuss with you tonight," said Lindsay. "Of course, we are considering other Dallas-area catering companies. Unless something drastic changes, we've already decided that Dallas will be our location because it seems to be such a popular venue these days. But your friend Margeaux has already sent us photos of you and told us so much about you. We were hoping that the bond of your friendship mixed with the intrigue of Pepper's social connections and prominence would come across on camera and make for an interesting reality show."

Pepper was sitting up even straighter—if that were possible—and beaming. Sydney was wide-eyed, mouth agape. A.J. was all-knowing smiles, like the cat who'd captured the mouse. How she had been able to keep this news to herself was a testament to her ironclad strength and willpower.

"So, what do you say?" Lindsay asked. "Would you like to hear more?"

Everyone nodded.

"How long have you been keeping this little gem from us, missy?" she demanded from A.J. with mock exasperation—her good nature was sparkling in her eyes.

A.J. cocked her head to the side. "Oh, for nearly three weeks. I didn't want to say anything until we were sure everything was going to pan out."

Lindsay cut in. "Really, it's our fault. Carlos and I have been trying to nail down a commitment from the network and sponsorships—both of which have been hurry-up-and-wait endeavors.

But finally, *finally,* we reached a meeting of the minds two days ago. This was the first chance that we had to fly in and meet with you. We did not even know we were going to be here until this morning."

Reminiscent of a shy schoolgirl, Sydney held up her hand. "May I please just clarify?" Her British accent sounded so proper. "You are interested in us? In putting us on the telly?"

Lindsay smiled the dazzling smile that had surely helped make her the food TV goddess she was.

"Absolutely," Carlos assured. "Of course, first we'd like to see how the synergy between the four of you works on camera. And, as I mentioned, we are interviewing a couple of other talent prospects, but I can say with a fair amount of certainty that Celebrations, Inc. looks very promising."

Sydney seemed to perk up and get stars in her eyes, but as the implications dawned on Caroline, she felt the color drain from her cheeks. If her father had taken issue with her photo appearing on page 3 of the local business journal, what would he say about the possibility of her appearing on national TV?

Even more important, she didn't know how she

felt about television cameras following her around and broadcasting her every move on national TV.

"So, the show is about a day in the life of a catering company, right?" she asked.

Lindsay nodded.

"And how exactly do Pepper, Sydney and I fit in?"

Lindsay smiled and blinked as if Caroline had just told a joke and Lindsay was trying very hard to understand the punch line but didn't quite get it.

"Caroline, since you're the pastry chef for Celebrations, Inc., we'd want to film you baking and working your sweet magic."

Okay...at midnight...in my condo kitchen...after I get home from the office...in sweatpants and a ponytail. Oh, no. This doesn't sound like a very good idea.

She shot a panicked glance at A.J., who, judging by the look on her face, seemed to be reading her mind and shooting back a telepathic, *This is important to me. Please just go with it.*

It *was* important—on so many levels. The publicity alone would put the catering company on the most-sought-after list. Plus she could tell how much A.J. wanted this, which was probably why she had not given her friends too many details before she gathered everyone.

Caroline could understand how Pepper, with her socialite reputation and connection among Dallas's elite, fit into a TV show, but Sydney's position as an occasional server and part-time PR rep and Caroline's place as a part-time baker and very part-time financial adviser…that did not seem like it would make for compelling viewing.

Caroline felt as if it was all coming at her a little too fast. Test shots, possible pilots, the fact that Lindsay and Carlos had been discussing her friends and her and Celebrations, Inc. for a few weeks and they'd had no idea. It was all a little overwhelming.

She was afraid her tendency to overthink things might cost the others this opportunity. So she excused herself to go to the restroom and the others joined in animated conversation, tossing around ideas of where they might shoot and potential parties that were coming up.

Yes, it was all just a little too much too fast for Caroline's whirling mind. The last thing she expected was to find Pepper on her heels, following her to the little girls' room.

"Can I talk to you for just a minute?" she asked. She glanced over her shoulder as if making sure they were truly alone.

Caroline was surprised that Pepper would tear

herself away from such exciting talks, but not nearly as flummoxed as she was when Pepper said, "I got a call from my father this morning after he saw the article in the *Journal*."

Again, she frowned and glanced around, ensuring they were alone.

Surely Harris Merriweather had not taken issue with his daughter being in the public eye. If ever there was a daddy's girl, it was Pepper. Even as busy as her father was, running a billion-dollar corporation, he doted on his daughter. Whatever made Pepper happy made Harris Merriweather happy. And this article had certainly delighted Pepper.

Yet for some reason, Pepper seemed uncharacteristically speechless.

"Is everything okay?"

"I don't know," said Pepper. "I'm not sure. I mean, I hope so, because I think Drew is a fabulous guy.... But, honey, when my dad called this morning after seeing the article in the paper, he warned me away from Drew. He said that the guy was bad news and suggested that we all stay clear of him."

Chapter Nine

A few days later, Caroline still wasn't sure if it was the bombshell that Pepper had dropped that had thrown her off her game as Carlos and Lindsay filmed the test shots that night they all had met at the Celebrations, Inc. kitchen, but she had felt as stiff as a frozen dish towel in front of the camera.

When Carlos and Lindsay brought out their camcorder to film reference footage of the Celebrations, Inc. kitchen and building—shots in which the women of Celebrations, Inc. were supposed to act "natural" Caroline clammed up. All she could think about was Harris Merriweather's warning about Drew. Pepper had been too busy to get together, and this was a conversation Caroline wanted to have face-to-face, not over the phone. So, she'd been left to stew and overthink the matter. Her tension came across on camera in sharp contrast to the way Pepper, A.J. and Sydney had hammed it up. Caroline didn't want her blue mood to bring them down—even though that might not even be in the realm of possibilities. They were naturals, while Caroline had never felt so lackluster and clunky in her entire life. It was as if she couldn't get out of her own way.

Even so, apparently her self-conscious appearance had not cost her friends the job, because one week to the day later, A.J. called with the good news that Carlos and Lindsay had made a formal offer to contract Celebrations, Inc. and the four friends as the stars of their new reality TV show, aptly titled *Celebrations, Inc.*

The four of them were meeting tonight after Sydney and Caroline got off work for a celebratory toast—and to look over the contract, which the attorneys for Epicurean Traveler had overnighted to A.J.

They were all meeting Sydney in the lobby of the Texas Star building in downtown Dallas and planned to walk to a local restaurant that offered a nice workweek happy hour.

As Caroline walked toward A.J. and Pepper—who were already waiting in the slick chrome-and-marble lobby, laughing and talking animatedly—she could feel their energy and exuberance across the lobby, and her heart sank.

How could she tell them that she really did not want this television gig? Really, all she wanted was to bake her cakes for the catering company and enjoy her new life with Drew. She had finally found the peace that she wanted; she'd finally found the courage to stand up to her father and put him and Coopersmith & Bales on notice that an all-consuming corporate life wasn't what she wanted for her future.

Now, *this*—a life in the public eye. It was bound to change everything.

Pepper and A.J. waved when they saw Caroline walking across the lobby. She bolstered herself, put on her best smile and waved back. They looked so happy. Now wasn't the time to tell them that she was having second thoughts.

But it was time to talk to Pepper about what she'd said about Drew. That was exactly what she planned to do once she got Pepper alone.

In the meantime, she decided that she would

feel out the situation with the TV show and see if, perchance, this didn't have to be a package deal. If, say, the show could go on with the three of them. She still had her job at Coopersmith & Bales. Even though she was freeing herself up to make more time to bake, she would still have the nine-to-five obligation—and occasionally even more hours.

"I hope you're ready to celebrate," said Pepper as Caroline walked up to them. Pepper set down a large shopping bag she was carrying and enfolded Caroline in an exuberant hug.

"I am so excited, I'm just about to die," she squealed. "Isn't this just about the best thing to happen to us in…well, it's just the best thing ever!"

"It is very exciting," Caroline said. And it was…in theory. Just not for her.

She changed the subject. "You look cute." Pepper was wearing a black-and-white skirt that was fitted at the stomach and then flared, hitting just above the knees. She had paired it with a black silk sweater and black patent stiletto heels that made her already tall, thin figure look graceful and willowy. A braid of large pearls and chains completed the ensemble. It was very Chanel-like.

Caroline turned and hugged A.J., too. "I am

so happy for you," she said to her friend, giving her a genuine smile despite the sinking feeling weighing her down inside. "You have worked so hard getting this company off the ground, and now with this new opportunity, it's going to soar."

The petite blonde crossed her arms over the red wool jacket she was wearing. She worried a strand of pearls at her neck, and Caroline thought she sensed a note of uncertainty in the usually confident woman.

"Is everything all right?" Caroline asked.

A sincere smile spread across A.J.'s pretty face, and she waved off Caroline's question. "Of course it is. I guess now that everything is sinking in, I have a bunch of questions. Mainly about how to keep the catering company a legitimate, working company in the midst of the television frenzy."

Not that misery loved company, but Caroline had to admit it made her feel better seeing A.J. a little taken aback, asking real-life questions rather than getting swept away by the hoopla. It felt good not to be the only realist in the group.

Pepper's situation allowed her to flit. When you were the daughter of one of the wealthiest men in America, that station afforded you more leeway than, say, those who were bound by a budget.

Both A.J. and Caroline came from means that

would never leave them starving and homeless, but another bond that she and A.J. shared was that each was driven to make it on her own, separate from the ties and obligations of family money.

"Oh, don't pay any attention to A.J.," Pepper teased. "You know how she hates change. It's just going to take a bit of time for her to get her head wrapped around the idea of what this really means for her future."

She turned to A.J. "Honey, you may have to hire on additional staff, but this show is going to have everyone in the Southeast lining up at our door. Don't you worry. As Celebrations, Inc.'s resident party planner and booking hostess, I will make sure that the staff and I have you booked into the next decade."

Caroline's left brow shot up and she looked at A.J. "That's her new title? Since when?"

A.J. chuckled and shrugged. "If that's what she wants to call herself, it's fine with me."

Pepper clapped her hand. "We all need titles. How else will our audience know what our roles are on the show?"

A.J. and Caroline exchanged a smile. The only thing that was certain was that Pepper was born to be in the public eye, and that was one of the things that was going to be a huge bright spot on the show. Unlike herself. Caroline had another wide-awake nightmare of freezing up or falling down or dropping a cake as the camera was turned on her. Okay, so it wasn't going to be live TV, but these reality shows thrived on exploiting the sensational. Because, let's face it, no one wanted to see the ho-hum. They wanted the Sturm und Drang.

Lord knew Caroline had had enough Sturm und Drang in the year that she had helped her sister plan her wedding. Now that it was finally her time for love, was it so bad that she didn't want it to unfold in the midst of a three-ring circus?

Even worse…now that she had fallen in love with Drew, what if Harris Merriweather ended up having legitimate dirt on him? Her stomach knotted. She had to clear this up once and for all.

"I need to visit the little girls' room," Caroline said. "Pepper, come with me. A.J., would you mind waiting here for Sydney?"

"Not at all," A.J. said. "But hurry back. The minute y'all walk away she'll probably show up."

"In that case," Pepper said, "let's start walking."

Once they were out of A.J.'s earshot, Caroline cut to the chase. She was tired of writing it off one minute and fearing the worst the next.

"Okay, so, the other night when we were meeting with Carlos and Lindsay, you mentioned something about your father warning you away from Drew."

Pepper sighed. "Oh, that? I'm sorry if that upset you— Have you been worrying about that since then?"

Caroline reached out and nudged her arm. "Of course I've been worrying. I…I'm really beginning to have feelings for him."

The early-evening sun poured in through the glass atrium, casting everything in a warm, golden glow. Even so, Caroline shivered.

Pepper shrugged. "Oh, honey, I'm sorry you've been worrying. I probably shouldn't have said anything because after I thought about it… My father is a businessman. When things don't go his way he gets…upset. He tends to see the worst in people. I really have no idea why he said it. Maybe he was put off by something Drew wrote about him or Texas Star, which seems plausible, if you think about it… We could go up and ask him if you want?"

Another chill zinged through Caroline. The thought of descending upon Harris Merriweather uninvited made Caroline think of Dorothy and company approaching the great and powerful Oz.

Only the glimpse behind the curtain might just prove to be more than she wanted to know about Drew.

Still, sticking her head in the sand would not make the truth disappear.

Suddenly, what she needed to do became crystal clear.

"I need to ask Drew," she said.

Pepper nodded. "That would probably be the best place to start. There are always two sides to a story. And somewhere in the middle is the truth."

Caroline chuckled. "You're absolutely right."

In the past, "truth" meant getting close. Getting close meant risk of rejection. Even thinking about it made a fear so large swell up inside of her it nearly swept her away. But in the time it took Caroline and Pepper to finish their business and get back to where A.J. was still waiting—alone— Caroline had a new resolve.

She had to talk to Drew.

A.J. glanced at her watch. "I wonder what's taking Sydney so long? Pepper, should we use your influence to go up there and break her out of jail?"

"Hell, no," she drawled. "This is as close as I want to get to the mouth of the Texas Star beast. Daddy might try to put me to work up there or…

something else. Look at what happened to Caroline when she got stuck in the family business flytrap."

They all laughed—even Caroline, despite the fact that Pepper's attempt to be funny had actually struck a little too close to home for comfort.

Because even though she was putting on a good-natured face over her discomfort, Pepper's comment sparked a legitimate concern in Caroline.

Pepper motioned to an arrangement of chairs and small tables set around a planter. "Come on, let's go over here and sit down and wait for her." They all went over and took a seat.

"I know they've said the premise of the show is they simply want to follow us around and tape us as we work—a-day-in-the-life sort of thing—but any show that's worth watching is based on conflict. That's what keeps people glued to the tube."

She paused, letting her words sink in a moment, hoping they'd already been pondering the same thing that had been niggling in the back of her mind since day one, when the possibility for the show even presented itself.

Nobody spoke. Her two friends simply sat and stared at her expectantly as if they wanted her to continue.

"I don't mean to be the buzz kill, but I really worry about how the producers are going to… come up with that conflict."

Continued blank stares.

"No, think about it," Caroline continued. "Haven't you seen those *Real Housewives* shows? Come on, admit it, you know you've seen at least one episode." When they still weren't saying anything, Caroline waved away the analogy.

"All they do is fight. And if there isn't something real for them to fight over, it seems like they create something. I guess I'm a little concerned about not letting this affect our friendship. The three of us, especially. We've known each other all our lives. I wouldn't hesitate a minute to sacrifice a life in the limelight to ensure that nothing comes between us."

A.J.'s eyes flashed. "I can promise you that I will not allow anything to come between us. If it makes you feel better, before we sign the contracts, I will make sure we have it in writing that our friendship will not be fodder for conflict."

Caroline did not want to burst her friend's bubble, but she wasn't so sure the producers were going to be very receptive about letting the talent dictate the direction of the show.

But for the sake of not starting a real-life argument, she said, "Okay, so the conflict doesn't come from us as friends and coworkers. Where is the conflict that keeps the viewers watching going to come from?"

"Oh, Caroline, you're so dramatic." Pepper sighed and picked up the shopping bag she had been carting around. "I think *you're* going to be a good source for drama and conflict."

Caroline clucked her tongue, taking issue with the backhanded…compliment? Really, it was more of an insult. This was precisely the type of thing she did not want aired on camera. She looking like the stick in the mud, while Pepper tossed barbs for comedic effect.

No, this wasn't going to work at all.

Pepper continued as if she had not just verbally upbraided Caroline. "I was going to wait until we were having drinks, but Sydney is so late. Where is she? I'm going to have to leave here pretty soon. But anyway, as a token of our friendship, *annnd* in celebration of this new opportunity, I have a present for you. Well, I have one for me, too, actually. They're for all of us. So that we match…"

She opened the shopping bag and handed Caroline and A.J. shirt-size boxes.

"Open them," she insisted. "They're Celebrations, Inc. aprons. I had them specially made for us. For the show."

Before anyone could remove the paper and ribbon from her box, Caroline spied Sydney exiting the elevators on the other side of the lobby.

"Oh, good, there she is," she said.

Pepper stood up and waved. "Sydney! Here we are."

That's when they noticed that Sydney was crying, and that two uniformed guards, their arms full of boxes, were escorting her toward the door.

Chapter Ten

The layoffs were yet another piece to the puzzle of the Texas Star story that Bia was piecing together. Although Drew had completely removed himself from that project, he was still editor of the *Journal* and therefore responsible for the rest of the content of each week's paper.

Bia had taken to giving him vague reports apprising him of where things stood: *we're getting hotter or colder; thumbs-up or thumbs-down on the progress.*

He trusted her reporting instincts and her judgment, but so far she had not indicated that she had found anything substantial enough to write about.

As Drew lived day by day in the safe haven he'd created of *Texas Star don't ask, don't tell,* he was falling more in love with Caroline every day.

For some reason she was hesitant about the Celebrations, Inc. television opportunity. When she asked for his advice, he told her he thought she would be a natural on television and that he thought she should seize the opportunity.

"But I'm so stiff on camera," she lamented. "I just don't know if it can work. I guess I'm afraid of embarrassing myself and letting my friends down." And what if she was such a weak link that she ended up being voted off the island? *Okay,* she was mixing up her reality TV metaphors—what it all boiled down to was she didn't want to risk the rejection.

"And how could you do that? I don't see how it would be possible for you to embarrass yourself or let your friends down. Everyone has faith in you. They want you to be a part of this project. They need you to be a part of this project. I think you need to go for it."

"It's just weird, thinking about your life playing out on TV," Caroline answered. "I mean, think about it. It could even involve you. It will involve us. Do you want to make cameo appearances on the show?"

He hadn't thought about that. But the fact that she was thinking of the show in the context of him, that he was now a real part of her life, felt good. It felt solid. *They* felt solid. But then the damned dark shadows of the implications of *what if* set in. What if Bia's story took off? What if Coopersmith & Bales were involved?

What if they weren't?

What if this was just his way of covering his own insecurities? That maybe, in fact, he wouldn't want his life to play out in the public eye? One of the things he loved the most about being a journalist was that he was the one who investigated others. He turned the spotlight on people and places and corrupt corporations with sketchy business practices and stonewalling reflexes. Other than his byline that appeared with the story or his credit listed on the paper's masthead, he remained largely anonymous. His *person* did anyway, even if his name might be known or cursed by scores of people who were unhappy about what he wrote about them. Just because Caroline was going to be on television didn't mean he had to be, too. Maybe that was the biggest double standard of all—that

he was pushing her to do something that he himself was uncomfortable doing.

But Caroline wasn't fully on board with the opportunity. Yet he was subtly nudging her in the
direction of the show. It was a position that most
people would gladly rearrange their lives to take
advantage of—and whether or not to trade in her
old job at Coopersmith & Bales seemed precisely
to be Caroline's dilemma.

She had reminded him that to be available for
taping and the production schedule and the various appearances that the show's publicist was
planning for the show, she would need to take a
leave of absence from her job at C & B. But then
something shifted. It had almost seemed like she
was beginning to consider the possibilities.

Because the other night when Drew had been
over at Caroline's helping her bake an order of va-
nilla bean cake with a chocolate raspberry mousse
filling for a Celebrations, Inc. event, she had said,
"My father still hasn't come to terms with the fact
that I won't be accepting the senior partner position. He'll flip when he finds out I'm quitting altogether to do this."

Drew had smiled. "So, it sounds like you've
made a decision?"

She'd stopped mixing the cake batter that she had been stirring, her spoon poised in midair. "I suppose I need to talk to my father so that we can come to a meeting of the minds before his retirement party next week. And there's something I need to talk to you about, too." She looked down at the bowl of batter as if gathering her thoughts

"Sure," he said. "Ask me anything."

He purposely tried to keep his voice light, because she looked as if she were struggling with something. He braced himself, but still managed to keep his smile in place.

"The other night when we were at the catering offices meeting, at that first meeting with Carlos and Lindsay, Pepper mentioned that there might be some bad blood between you and her father, Harris Merriweather."

Who in Texas didn't have bad blood with Harris Merriweather?

But he couldn't say it quite so baldly to the best friend of Harris Merriweather's daughter.

"I don't know if you'd call it *bad blood* so much as you'd call it a difference of opinion as what is newsworthy and what's…let's see how can I translate what Mr. Merriweather called it without offending your sensibilities."

He winked at her. Caroline was a strong

woman. She could handle it, he simply didn't care to use that particular brand of language in her presence.

"I believed it was something to the tune of *bull hockey*." He smiled and shrugged. "Well, there was definitely *bull* in the sentiment. One thing you need to know about me is if I do my job right, I'm not always going to please everyone. If I tried to do that then there would be no fair and unbiased news to report. Does that make sense? But other than falling out of favor with Harris Merriweather, I can assure you that I don't have a criminal record and I work very hard to keep my bad habits down to a manageable roar."

She laughed, and her cheeks seemed to radiate a new, rosy glow. "Well, in that case, will you be my date to my father's retirement party?"

"I would be honored," he said. "Look, something just dawned on me. I have a hunch that once you get everything ironed out with your father and you make him understand that this is important to you—or more so, that a career at Coopersmith & Bales is not what you want—I believe you'll loosen up on camera."

He walked over and put his arms around her. "The camera loves you, and so do I."

* * *

In passing, when Caroline happened to mention that her father was retiring and the party was coming up soon, Carlos and Lindsay had latched onto the idea that the party, which would take place at the Regency Cypress Plantation and Botanical Gardens just outside of Celebration, would be the perfect place to film the first episode of the pilot.

The stately old estate had been a working sugar plantation in the early-nineteenth century. Since then, it had become a much sought-after venue for special occasions—and the first location for the new television show that would feature Celebrations, Inc.

Carlos and Lindsay had offered to approach her father about it, but Caroline had curtailed that in a hurry. It was time she talked to her father. This was as good a time as any. She just needed to bite the bullet and do it.

She had made a lunch reservation at Manuel's, and to her relieved surprise he made himself available. Of course, she had said she wanted to talk to him about her future with Coopersmith & Bales, and she thought he was probably holding out hope for a positive outcome. That made her nervous.

You're thirty-three years old. It's time you started living life on your own terms. Those terms include leaving the darkness of the firm, taking your place in the sun as you costar in a reality television show and introducing Drew to your father.

The thought unleashed the butterflies in her stomach. She realized the butterflies swooped more at the thought that she would be telling her father about Drew—that he was someone special in her life.

When was the last time she had told her father that she was serious about a man? Never. She never had.

That Drew would be by her side at the retirement party and from there on after in her life made her feel stronger than she had ever felt before.

Maybe it was the confident way she presented everything: her decision to leave, the television opportunity, that she was finally fully and soundly head-over-heels in love. But for the first time she felt like her father actually heard her.

He sipped his water, studying her over the glass. "You and this catering company you've invested in are going to be on television?"

She cleared her throat. "Yes, we are. We start filming in two weeks."

He nodded as he looked at the menu, and for a

moment, she wondered if he was still listening or if his mind had wandered off to wherever it went when he tuned her out.

So she looked at the menu, too.

"What's the shooting schedule like?"

Oh, he's still listening.

"It's going to be tight. The plan is to shoot the pilot and then if the network is happy with it—and it gets good reviews from the areas where the pilot is test marketed—we will jump right into taping a first season."

Again, he nodded rather absently as he stared at his menu. He didn't say another word until after the server took their orders and refilled their water and iced-tea glasses.

When they were alone again, he said, "So, are you giving me your two weeks' notice? Is that why you asked me to have lunch with you today?"

"In a sense, I guess I am. Of course, I will type up a formal letter of resignation tonight and file it with the human resources department."

Inwardly, she was kicking herself for not having thought to bring a letter of resignation with her. That would've made it more formal. More final. But at least he was being nice.

"I suppose you're going to tell me opportunities like this don't come along every day," he said.

"I beg your pardon?" She wasn't quite sure what he meant. *Please don't start lecturing me about foolish, impulsive moves.* She knew a reality television show wasn't a career move that would last a lifetime or serve as a stepping stone to help her reach bigger and better things, but it was important to her. She just wished he could see for once that sometimes the impractical things were worth it if they were important enough. She was just gathering her thoughts to tell him that she would be self-sufficient. She wouldn't ask him for money or even expect him to give her her old job back at Coopersmith & Bales. She understood that this decision was binding.

"I can understand why taking the television opportunity is important to you," he said. "Opportunities like that don't come along every day. The only thing is, I can't accept your resignation."

She sat there and blinked at him. Was he really going to make this so hard? Did everything have to be a struggle?

"How about if we call it an indefinite leave of absence instead? You can come back if and when you're ready. Really, you'd be doing that more for me than for yourself, because I have no doubt that you will be successful at whatever you choose to do. Let's just call the leave of absence in lieu of resignation your retirement present to me, okay?"

His smile let her know that yes, indeed, she had heard him correctly. Or, more important, that *he* had finally heard *her*.

Who'd have known Charles Coopersmith would have been so full of surprises? Drew thought as he walked into the man's retirement party on the arm of his daughter.

After Caroline's lunch with her father, she had floated the idea of using his retirement party as the backdrop for the pilot. To everyone's astonishment, he'd actually agreed. Of course, that meant that not only did Celebrations, Inc. have to cater the event, but it meant that the four women were also guests. A.J. and Caroline had done all the prep work on the savory and sweet foods, but they had to hire staff to execute and serve.

Caroline looked beautiful tonight in a form-fitting blue gown that hugged her curves in all the right places. She and Pepper seemed to be right in their element mixing and mingling with the guests, but A.J. and Sydney had removed themselves from the party for the most part and were spending a great deal of time in the kitchen.

Drew had been right about how once Caroline had gotten things straightened out with her father, she would be much more at ease on camera. Once they were inside and had made their initial rounds to greet people, Drew had stood on the sidelines watching Caroline, who seemed perfectly at ease—as if the television cameras weren't even there.

While he was glad that Caroline had wanted him by her side tonight, he had not fully realized that circulating among the guests would be quite similar to navigating a minefield. Case in point was when he spied Harold Grady, the opinionated family friend who had chewed out Drew on his first date with Caroline in downtown Celebration. Drew did his best to steer clear of him. And there was Harris Merriweather walking straight toward him.

These men were slick and savvy business moguls, Dallas's business elite. However, seeing Drew in a tux as a guest at an event like this took him out of context. No doubt the men must have looked at him and thought he looked vaguely familiar, then dismissed him as someone they'd simply met along the way. Merriweather walked right by Drew, doing a double take but continuing on to greet a distinguished-looking couple who were standing a few feet behind him.

It was odd being at an event like this and actually being on the guest list. Drew definitely felt out of his element. He had, actually, been given the right to write a story about Coopersmith's retirement and the taping of the show's pilot. And other media were there, of course, but in a more official capacity—some wearing their press credentials, others actively working with pen and notebook in hand or talking into a microphone as they recapped the event for news cameras.

Yes, tonight, Drew was definitely a fish out of water—actually, he was neither fish nor fowl. He was in love with a woman who belonged in a world that, to him, was a hotbed of scandal. Even though he was on the inside tonight, he was definitely the outsider gazing in.

After drinks and dinner, during which Drew and Caroline sat at the head table with her father and mother, Charles Coopersmith's friends and colleagues took turns roasting him. Interestingly, several used his daughter's new role on the show as fodder for their jokes, asserting that he had given up accounting to become a reality television star or to join his daughter in the catering business. There were several invitations to cater festivities—birthday parties, anniversary celebrations and New Year's Eve bashes.

At one point, he felt Caroline shift in her seat a little bit. It was a barely perceptible shift of posture, but he caught it and leaned down to whisper, "Are you okay? Do you want to go out and get some air?"

"Maybe in a few minutes," she said. "But right now I'm fine."

Then Drew felt the buzz of a text message come through. As inconspicuously as possible, he slid the phone out of his pocket and checked the message.

It was from Bia: *SOS! Please call me ASAP. Very important.*

Drew waited until the current speaker was finished and then excused himself to go out into the lobby to return her call.

She answered on the first ring. "Drew, thank God you called me back so fast. You're not going to believe this. I found someone from Texas Star who is willing to talk on the condition that he remain anonymous."

Chapter Eleven

Caroline had been disappointed that Drew had to leave before the roast was over, but he told her he had an emergency that couldn't wait. She had understood. Really, the party had been going on a little too long. People were taking cheap shots at her father, ribbing him about things that had more to do with her than him. She had found it a bit inappropriate but did the socially correct thing and kept her party smile firmly in place.

She was proud of herself for not once letting it slip.

Now that she was at home and she could relax,

she thought about how ironic it was that reality television would have loved a good cat fight over some of the things that were said tonight.

As she changed out of her gown and into a pair of comfortable slacks and a sweater set, she laughed to herself about the opportunities she could've taken. Of course, she hadn't and never would, because that just wasn't her style, but it was fun to think about it.

Maybe Celebrations, Inc. would bring a whole new level of class to reality TV. But the most important thing about tonight—besides giving her father a good send-off on his retirement journey—was that she had actually enjoyed herself. Granted, the roast was tedious and the social part was exhausting, but what she had loved about the evening was how at home she had felt as a part of the Celebrations, Inc. team. She had made the chocolate mousse that had been served for dessert and it had been beyond thrilling to watch people enjoy it.

Her only disappointment was that Drew had not been there at the end of the night to toast the show's success. Carlos and Lindsay had said because of the friendship dynamic and the glimpse that the quartet of friends provided into the Dallas area social arena, they could all but guarantee that there would be a first season and had given each of them a bottle of champagne to take home. She wished that Drew could've been there to celebrate with them.

She had an idea and glanced at her watch. It was eleven-fifteen. But it was a Wednesday night. Since she wasn't sure whether he was at home asleep by this point or was perhaps tied up with something that would not be conducive to answering the phone, she decided to text him.

Where are you, my love?

He texted her back right away. *Still at the office. I'm sorry. I miss you.*

Then she had an idea.

What in hell was Drew going to do now?

He sat in his office and read and then reread Bia's article. Her anonymous source had given her some damming inside information—stories about file shredding, about how the whole office would be in an uproar just before the facts and figures for the quarterly report were due and then, miraculously, not only would everything be fine, but Texas Star would be boasting a profit increase. This, said the source, was accomplished by padding numbers, shuffling accounts and falsifying records. In essence, Bia Anderson had proof positive, thanks to sensitive documents that the ex-employee had copied and stuck away for safe-keeping, that Texas Star was one gigantic shell game on the verge of collapse.

When the mammoth went down, it would not only bruise the Dallas-area economy, but thousands of innocent people would lose their life savings while a few of the Texas Star upper echelon—namely, Harris Merriweather—had been living large with his four mansions and fleets of cars, airplanes and yachts.

Drew felt lightheaded. He leaned forward and braced his head on his hands. He inhaled through his nose and out through his mouth noisily. Never before had he experienced something so bitter-sweet.

On one hand, this was a story that would put his small newspaper on the map. Hell, they were going to scoop the *Wall Street Journal*. It had journalistic prizes written all over it.

On the other hand, there was Caroline.

Oh, God, Caroline. How in the world was he going to make her understand that he had a journalistic duty to run this story? Reporters were the watchdogs of society. He would be guilty of negligence if he did not do his duty and publish Bia's article. Since it was Wednesday night, time was of the essence. They would go to press tomorrow. Friday, the article would hit the newsstands. They had to clear all the hurdles: Drew had read it—and it was a damn good story. It was going to nail Merriweather and his band of conniving criminals to the wall. Bia had called Coopersmith & Bales, but they weren't talking; the publisher of the *Journal* had read it and signed off; the *Journal*'s attorneys had looked it over to make sure it was free of potential legal hangnails. So far they had given it the green light. The only step left before they went to press was to get a statement from someone at Coopersmith & Bales, Texas Star's auditor of record. Of course, they weren't expecting the good folks at C & B to say much other than "no comment" but they had to give them a chance to speak. Bia had tried to get a hold of someone today but was told that the publicists were not available. She would have to call back tomorrow.

The administrative assistant who took the call had incorrectly assumed that Bia was calling for information about Charles Coopersmith's retirement. Bia did not correct her. She did not want to reveal her hand before she had a chance to talk to someone in person.

That would happen tomorrow. If not, they

would go to press with or without a statement from C & B.

The story was going to run and all hell was going to break loose. The best way for Drew to cut his losses with Caroline, to cushion the blow, would be to tell her. He *had* to tell her before it hit the stands and everything hit the fan.

So that meant he needed to talk to her tonight. Just as the thought had registered, his phone buzzed a text notification from Caroline.

Look out your window, it said.

He did. She was sitting in her car, a huge smile on her face, crooking her finger on her left hand in a *come here* motion and holding up a bottle of champagne with the other.

Because his brain was on overload with all the baggage of the Texas Star debacle, seeing her looking so happy, beckoning him to come outside and drink champagne with him threw him for a second. Then he remembered: she had no idea what was about to happen.

She has no idea that I'm about to break her heart. I love her so much, but I'm about to become the person she hates the most in the entire world.

He held up his phone, indicating that he was going to text her back.

I still have some work to do. Please come inside.

* * *

The guy was a workaholic. But that was one of the many things she loved about him—his dedication to the job and the way he was learning to balance work and time with her. He really had made a concerted effort to let his assistant editor take on some of the workload. That's why she understood when the occasional crisis—like tonight's—happened.

Too bad it had to be on the night of the party and the pilot taping. But she forgave him. And she wanted to make sure he understood that. Hence the bottle of champagne.

His office was on the first floor of a three-story office building. Though she'd driven by the place many times, it was the first time she'd ever been inside.

He met her at the door, looking tired and… stressed. Definitely not himself.

Uh-oh, had she made a mistake by showing up uninvited? She hugged him at the door, careful not to be too touchy-feely, since she didn't know who else was in the building with him.

Oh…should she have brought the champagne? That might be frowned on. Especially if he was in the middle of an emergency. Well, they didn't have to open it right now.

But he was definitely hugging her back. In fact, for a moment, it felt as if he did not want to let her go.

Oh, my gosh. Did someone die?

Something was definitely off-kilter.

"Is everything okay?" she asked when they finally pulled out of the hug.

He looked at her for a long moment. She could actually see the great effort he was making as he was thinking. Thinking very, very hard.

Finally, he just raked his hands into his hair and let out a low growl.

"My God, Drew, what's wrong? You're scaring me."

"Just come inside," he said, stepping back so she could walk around him into the *Journal*'s lobby. She looked around the sparsely decorated reception area as he locked the door. Her first impression was that the place was very…white. Scuffed white walls, white laminated reception desk, gray-white tile on the floors. It was obviously a place where function was valued over form. But that was okay.

The next thing she noticed was that the place was very quiet and empty.

"Come on." Drew motioned her past a large room that was broken up by at least a dozen cubicles. It boasted framed posters with motivational sayings on the wall and what looked like a giant spreadsheet with the words SALES GOALS printed across the top.

Ah, that must be where they kept the sales force.

They passed down a short hallway into a smaller room with six cubicles outside of a glass office.

"This has to be the infamous newsroom that I've heard so much about," she said, trying to lighten his mood.

Her heart sank when he did not crack a smile.

"Look, Drew, I can leave if it's a bad time. I don't want to keep you from your work. I probably should've called before I barged in on you."

"No, stay. Please," he said. This time he pressed his palms into his eyes before raking his hand through his hair. Obviously, that was his stress tic. It was really worrying her. "Just come in here. Into my office. Sit. Do you want some coffee or a soda or something?"

"No," she said as she followed him inside. "I just want you to tell me what's wrong. Because you are definitely not yourself."

He sat down at his desk and first looked at his

hands as if ordering his words. Then he looked at her.

She sat down, bracing herself for the bombshell he was obviously about to drop.

"Our managing editor, Beatrice Anderson, has been working on an investigative story for a few weeks now."

Caroline nodded. *So far, so good. That's what they do at a newspaper—research, write and publish stories.*

"Nothing out of the ordinary there."

He shook his head. "No, you don't understand. This story is very out of the ordinary and it's not good, Caroline. It's about Texas Star. Our evidence points to fraud."

It took a moment for his words to sink in. *Not good. Texas Star. Fraud.*

"Drew, what do you mean?"

"Exactly what I just said. We have evidence that Texas Star has been defrauding its investors."

Suddenly, as the implications of what he was saying began to sink in, she shook her head as if doing so could fend off his words. Those ugly words.

"No, it's impossible, because I've known Harris Merriweather my entire life. Pepper is one of my best friends. Do you realize that what you're saying is very damaging?"

"I know the implications. If we didn't have ironclad proof, you and I wouldn't be having this conversation right now."

"Whoa, whoa, whoa! Wait a minute. You say you have ironclad proof that there had been fraud?"

Drew nodded.

"Are you forgetting that Coopersmith & Bales is the auditor for Texas Star? Because if you're saying you have ironclad proof of fraud, you're either accusing us of covering it up or not knowing what the hell we're doing."

"Bia hasn't talked to anyone from your office yet. I wanted to talk to you and let you know what was going on before she calls tomorrow. I didn't want you to be blindsided."

Caroline leaned forward in her chair. "Am I supposed to thank you for that, Drew? You're basically accusing my family...no, you're accusing *me* of fraud. Do you realize that?"

"Caroline, I'm not."

"Yes, you are."

"Are you involved with the Texas Star account?"

She opened her mouth to say something, but

then she shut it again, blinking in obvious disbelief. "Well, no. That's not an account that I handle."

"Then how do you know what's going on with
them?"

She rolled her eyes. "I don't have to know
what's going on to be one hundred percent sure
that Coopersmith & Bales doesn't condone fraud-
ulent practices. That's as bad as me accusing you
of—"

"Hack reporting." He finished her sentence for
her. "Which is exactly what you're sitting right
there accusing me of."

He took a deep breath and seemed to regain
his composure. "Caroline, the paper's attorneys
have looked over our findings. We have uncovered enough evidence to substantiate our findings.
Texas Star is in big trouble."

He seemed to imply that Coopersmith & Bales
might be, too. Although he had the decency to not
come right out and say it.

"What is this evidence? I want to see it. I want
to read this story."

"I'm not the one investigating and writing the
piece. So it's not mine to give to you. If you want
to contact Bia tomorrow, you can ask her, but I
have to warn you that most reporters won't let

anyone but their editor read the story before it's printed."

Caroline sat there, blinking, trying regain her equilibrium. "Drew? How can this be happening?"

"I'm sorry. You have no idea how sorry I really am. Caroline, I love you. I would never do anything to purposely cause you or your family any pain. I'd never hurt Pepper purposely, either. That's why I'm telling you before you read it in the paper on Friday."

The bottom dropped out of her stomach. "Friday? As in the day after tomorrow?"

He nodded. "That's when it's going to run."

It was all starting to come into focus now. That first date when she'd mentioned that Sydney had said some things were wonky at Texas Star. Then he had access to inside info through Pepper and Sydney after she was laid off. "I am such a fool." She hadn't realized she'd said the words out loud, but the look on his face made her glad she did. "All along I thought you were seeing me because you cared. Drew, we agreed that anything I said when we were together—God, when we were in bed—was off the record. What, did you have a tape recorder going the entire time? Were you writing down everything I said and passing the notes on to your little assistant?"

He frowned and shook his head vehemently. "I know this isn't going to make you feel any better, but this story was not born from anything you said. Everything was always off the record when we were together. Caroline, you have to believe me when I promise you that this paper has been investigating Texas Star for a long time."

"And you expect me to believe that after all this time the pieces just magically fell into place once we started dating? That it wasn't because of the proximity you had to the daughters of both organizations that are being taken to task? Do you think I'm an idiot, Drew?"

He looked as if she'd slapped him. And at that moment, the wild angry beast in her that he had unleashed wished she could. That in itself scared her, because she abhorred violence.

But she felt so violated.

Used and violated.

She couldn't even wrap her mind around the fallout that this was going to cause—the dark shadows it would cast on Coopersmith & Bales; how it would stress her relationship with her father and Pepper; and the television show… The sponsors were probably already running to disassociate themselves from the scandal that was sure to reach much farther than the lowly *Dallas Journal of Business and Development.*

"I've been sitting here racking my brain trying to think of some way to convince you that I did not use you, that this story was in the works long before you and I were together."

"Save it, Drew." She stood up to leave.

Drew stood up, too, and moved between her and the door.

"No, Caroline, listen to me. Please. When we got the latest quarterly earnings statement from Texas Star, I gave it to Bia to look at. She's the one who noticed the discrepancies. She talked to someone on the inside who spilled everything. Things that you and Pepper would have no way of knowing. Things even I didn't know until I read the story. The minute Bia told me she was onto something at Texas Star, I recused myself from the project because loving you and working on the story would be a conflict of interest. I chose you over reporting this story. I have not even been involved in editing it. The only reason I read it is I have to sign off on every story before we go to press. I've told you a lot more than we ever reveal about our work before the paper is published. I shouldn't have said anything about our source." His face softened. He signed. "Will you please believe me when I tell you I'm sorry? I love you, and I never meant for this to hurt you. Or your family or Pepper."

He was so tall and imposing, and damn it all if she didn't find her mind remembering how he looked as he was making love to her, how well their bodies fit together and how his lips tasted. Now, those same lips were moving very fast, trying to convince her that he didn't use her to further himself, his career. So that he could look like the golden boy reporting the story of the century. God, and now even she was starting to think that she believed that the allegations he was going publish were true.

But then something he'd just said clicked.

"So, you have to sign off on every story?"

He nodded.

"What happens if you don't sign off on something?"

"I pull it and put something in its place. Like we did for the business profile when we featured Celebrations, Inc."

She put her hands on her hips and looked up at him, locking gazes, keeping her expression hard and unwavering. "So, if you wanted to, you could refuse to run the piece on Texas Star?"

He flinched and looked at her as if she had two heads. "I could pull a story if there was a substantial reason it shouldn't run. What are you suggesting, Caroline?"

"I'm *suggesting* that if you love me as much as you say you do, then you'll kill the story."

Again, he looked like she'd struck him, only this time her words had landed like a punch in the gut.

"That's not going to happen," he said. "There's nothing wrong with that story. It's one hundred percent true. We have the facts, figures and documents to back it up."

"Drew, let me make myself clear, since you obviously don't understand. If this story runs, it's going to hurt a lot of people I love. I am begging you to pull it. Unless you do, I will have no choice but to walk out of this office and out of your life for good."

"You're giving me an ultimatum?" he asked. "You want me to not do what's good and just and right? You want me to look the other way after Texas Star has defrauded their employees, their investors? These people are going to be left with nothing once the smoke clears. And you think that's okay?"

Now, she felt like *she* was the one who had

been punched in the gut. Why did it always have to end this way? Why did it always have to end? Period.

She felt herself choking up and knew that she had to get out of there. But once she walked away, her whole life was going to come tumbling down around her.

"I stand by the people I love, Drew. I cannot believe that a man like Harris Merriweather, a man I've known my entire life, is capable of the heinous acts you're accusing him of. And what's more, I will never believe that my father used the company my great-grandfather built from scratch to help him cover his tracks. So, I'll ask you one more time. If you love me, please pull the story."

Drew stood and walked to the door. His face was hard and angry. "Then I guess this is good-bye, Caroline. Because if you really loved me as deeply as I love you, there would be no way that you would ask me to disregard the truth."

Chapter Twelve

The next afternoon, Drew sat alone in his office. The Texas Star story was finished—with a firm "We never discuss client matters with the press," issued by Richard Bales. Apparently, Charles Coopersmith had left on a postretirement cruise early that morning and could not be reached for comment.

Drew hadn't heard from Caroline since he'd watched her walk out to her car and drive out of his life. Now, a pervading sense of numbness kicked in when he thought of her. He was glad. Because if not, he wouldn't be able to function.

He had to conduct business and get through the day, since work was all he had left.

Too bad this numbness couldn't block out thoughts of Caroline, too. And thoughts of her had been dogging him all day. Caroline in the kitchen; Caroline in the bedroom; something funny she'd said; an expression she'd make.

What was she doing today?

Had she talked to her father before he left on the cruise?

At least a dozen times today, he'd started to pick up the phone to call her and then remembered that last night, on her own volition, she'd walked out of his life for good.

How could he have loved someone who had no idea what he was about? What he was made of? How could he love someone who had so little regard for the truth?

A crescendo of laughter peaked and pulled him from his brooding. Through the glass walls of his office, he watched the rest of the staff celebrating their coup, the fact that they'd scooped all the financial newspapers—and more so that they'd finally dismantled "Stonewall," as they'd not so fondly taken to calling Harris Merriweather.

Bia popped open a bottle of champagne and was pouring it in paper cups and coffee mugs.

Drew watched the staff toast her. As they should. It was her moment. Moments like this were too few and far between. She deserved to bask in the glow.

It was as if he were watching a silent movie— shiny, happy people putting work aside for the moment, taking the last hour to celebrate Bia's victory.

He, on the other hand, still had work to do. The paper was ready to be emailed to the printer—all of this week's stories had been written and edited. The advertising had been placed. Everything that needed to be officially approved had been by all who officially signed off.

This week's edition was good to go.

Why, then, had he not sent it to the press? All he needed to do was push a button to send it on its way. Then, tomorrow morning, evidence of the staff's hard work would magically appear on newsstands, in mailboxes on desks and coffee tables all across Dallas.

Interesting that he had not yet heard anything from Texas Star. Surely by now they knew that the story would run tomorrow. Drew had braced himself for a threatening call or even a cease and desist from the energy company's legal counsel. But he had not heard a peep.

Until Drew pressed Send on that email, there was still a chance in the universe that he and Caroline could be. But once he'd detonated this week's issue, their relationship would be officially over.

The email was up on his monitor. The mouse was in his hand. His finger hovered over the mouse. All he had to do was click.

Click. It would be just that easy. If only he could unstick his frozen finger.

The sound of someone tapping on the glass made him jump. He looked up to see Bia holding up two coffee mugs, asking in pantomime if he wanted one.

He waved her away, pointing to his computer and shrugging. His own way of pantomiming that he was still working. Actually, *masquerading* was probably a better word, but Bia didn't need to know that.

As she turned away, Drew's gaze landed on the bottle of champagne that Caroline had brought in last night and forgotten in her hurry. It stood like a sentinel keeping watch over him. Taunting him... *Don't push that button. Before you do, think of all you're giving up.*

But if he didn't, anything he gained would never make up for the integrity and self-respect he lost.

In one aggressive rush, all the anger that had been hidden behind the numbness broke through. Caroline didn't love him. If she did, then she would never have given him the ultimatum to kill the story or lose her forever.

Because by simply saying that, she'd lost him.

His index finger came down hard on the mouse.

The pin had been pulled from the grenade.

Sleep and baking had always been Caroline's defense against a dark night of the soul. When life's problems got too big or too hard, all she had to do was bake a cake, and after that was done, she would close her eyes, and for a few blissful hours she could cast off her troubles.

So what was a girl to do after baking six cakes, and still sleep would not come to her? What any sensible girl would do—she enlisted the help of her friends.

Despite the fact that she was approaching thirty-six hours of sleep deprivation—and she'd comforted herself with so much cake that even her sweat pants were beginning to feel tight—she had asked her friends to meet her for dinner. A.J. had offered to cook, saying she had some recipes she was dying to try. Eager to get the contraband out of the house, Caroline had offered to bring dessert.

The girls of Celebrations, Inc. hadn't yet gotten word on whether the pilot had passed the muster. They were a few days—maybe even a week or ten days—away from getting that news. And, oh, how she could use some good news right about now.

But first she had to face a little more bad weather before she could hope for brighter days. She hadn't yet told Pepper about the article, and she owed it to her friend to tell her the news herself rather than letting her read about it the same way the masses would.

She'd invited Pepper over for a drink before the dinner at A.J.'s. Caroline just hoped that Pepper would still be speaking to her after she told her everything.

After showering and dressing in a pair of black wool pants and a gray silk button-down, Caroline opened a bottle of merlot and set out a block of Irish cheddar cheese that she'd picked up at the market the other day. It was a cheese that Drew had introduced her to, and she'd gotten this block for them to share.

A lump formed in her throat, and she chastised herself for being ridiculous. How could she be upset over a man who would toss her best friend and family under the bus for a few moments of professional glory?

Still, she'd allowed herself to care for him, and the empty place that he had once occupied so well felt like a big, gaping hole. It would just take a while for the wound to heal, she reminded herself.

She poured herself some wine and went into the living room, doing her best to push thoughts of Drew into the dark recesses of her mind. Right now, she needed to concentrate on how in the world she was going to break the news to Pepper. The mere thought made her a little queasy.

Ten minutes later, Pepper arrived, all smiles and hugs. She obviously knew nothing about the situation at hand. They sat at Caroline's kitchen table, drinking wine and making small talk about everything under the sun until, inevitably, the conversation turned to Drew.

"Where is Clark Kent on this fine Thursday night?" Pepper asked.

Hearing the nickname that Pepper had bestowed on him made Caroline's heart clench, or maybe it was a physical reaction to what she was about to tell her friend. "I have no idea."

She took a long sip of wine, hoping that she seemed more nonchalant than she felt.

Pepper's face fell. "Caroline…? What's going on honey?"

Caroline felt her composure begin to slip. So she didn't speak for a good thirty seconds while her armor hardened again. Finally, she took a deep breath and said what she needed to say.

"I'm afraid that your father was right when he told you to warn me away from Drew."

Caroline clamped her lip shut and bit the inside of her cheeks to keep the tears from leaking. The great pains she was taking to hold them in made her nose burn and her cheeks hurt.

Pepper leaned in. "What happened? Tell me everything," she insisted in a low, dish-me-the-goods voice.

Tell me everything.

Pepper's words, the wine, the cheese and crackers…it was déjà vu—flashback to that night after Caroline had first met Drew. Only it had been a Monday night. Tonight was Thursday. And back then the whole world had seemed bright and shiny and full of new possibilities.

Now, here she sat trying to find the words to tell her friend that the man she and Pepper had celebrated with so much gusto really was as big a louse as Harris Merriweather had foretold.

How could she be so stupid?

"Pepper, I have to tell you something, and I just don't quite know how to say it."

"Oh, God, please don't tell me you're pregnant and he's left you."

She wished it were something that simple. At least a baby would be loved and wanted, even if single parenthood would not be ideal.

"No, I'm not pregnant." And her prospects for a family of her own had never looked bleaker. Because now not only was she heartbroken, but she didn't trust her own judgment when it came to men. How had her picker strayed so far off course? Then again, she reminded herself, beginning a relationship with a one-night stand hadn't exactly set the stage for a lifetime of bliss.

She tried to convince herself of this, but something about it rang hollow. Maybe it was because she was leaving out the part where she'd actually fallen in love with him.

"I think Drew may have used me to get to you for a story for his newspaper."

Pepper frowned. "What are you talking about?"

She told her friend about the story that was due to come out tomorrow. Pepper was silent for a long minute. Caroline could see the wheels turning, but she didn't sense any anger in her friend.

"So, did you actually tell him something that helped him shape the story?"

"Well, no. Not exactly. I mean, because we were dating, he was around you and Sydney. Sydney lost her job and because of that, one of the reporters at the paper went on a witch hunt until she found someone who would talk."

"But it wasn't Sydney, right?"

"No, not as far as I know. But I really don't think so."

"And you say that he didn't write the story himself?"

Caroline shook her head. "In fact, he said he recused himself from the story once he…once he…"

"Honey, what is it?"

"Once he fell in love with me."

The words seemed to resonate in the air.

Pepper blew out a breath. "I know you're not going to want to hear this, but I'm going to say it anyway. I have no idea what the article is about—Daddy is always dealing with press who seem to come preprogrammed to believe that any very rich man didn't get that way by being an honest man." She shrugged. "I don't get in the middle of my father's business dealings. It's something that's never interested me, and thank God my dad isn't like yours and thinks I need to carry on his legacy.

But I digress. What I wanted to say was I believe that Drew loves you. Call me a hopeless romantic, but there is something about the way that guy looks at you that nearly causes everything in his wake to spontaneously combust."

Caroline was doing her best to concentrate on how well her friend was handling the news, rather than the part that she was reinforcing that Caroline had probably just let the love of her life get away.

Then she came full circle, back to the original point—that they were in this mess because... because...

"Then you don't think he used me to get the story?"

Pepper pulled a face. "Did you or did you not know that he was a newspaper man when you set your sights on him? Rhetorical question." She winked at her friend. "Of course you knew. It would've been one thing if he'd been masquerading around here pretending to be something he wasn't, lurking in the shadows, hiding the fact that he was a news man. But he was pretty up front with it."

"So, Pepper, what are you saying? That if someone wrote a potentially damaging story about your family, that you could just say it's all in a day's work and bring him home to Daddy?"

Pepper threw back her blond head and laughed. "Hell, no. Are you kidding? My father would eat him for lunch. What I'm saying is if I found a guy who looked at me the way Drew looks at you and he was just doing his job, then I'd see if there was a way that we could somehow meet in the middle. Or at some secret place so Daddy wouldn't kill him. My God, if you hadn't already ruined Clark Kent for all the other women who come after you, I'd be out there trying to salvage him for myself. Except I don't want your sloppy seconds."

For the first time since Drew had dropped the bomb that had detonated their relationship, Caroline laughed. Pepper either had the right attitude or she was completely out of touch with reality.

Caroline decided she would wait until Pepper read the article before she decided which. In the meantime, there was someone else she needed to talk to, to figure out whether she should reopen the conversation with Drew.

Chapter Thirteen

Richard Bales only made Caroline wait twenty minutes before he would see her. She justified the wait because she didn't have an appointment. She had just walked in and told his administrative assistant that she needed to speak with him.

When she finally walked into his office, she felt like Dorothy when she was ultimately granted a meeting with the great and powerful Oz. She wondered if he'd make her go steal the Wicked Witch's broomstick before he gave her any answers.

Bales was talking on the phone, turned around in his desk chair with his back to her.

She coughed to make him aware that she was standing there. He turned around and motioned for her to take a seat in one of the chairs in front of his desk. As she did, she wished she hadn't warned him so that she could have eavesdropped a little on his conversation. She was such a rule follower, but the conversation didn't sound like it was anything important anyway. She had actually been hoping he might be talking to Harris Merriweather. That they had been discussing the article that had appeared that morning above the fold on the front page of the *Journal.*

No luck. She'd just have to bring it up herself.

"Caroline, how lovely to see you, my dear."

"My dear"? Really? Would he have called you that if you had taken over for your father?

He smiled a toothy smile, and her next thought was that he was way too cheery. Had he not seen the article?

"How's the catering business? Or should I ask, how is the reality TV business treating you? Did you come to ask for your old job back?"

"First of all, I'm only on a leave of absence, I didn't quit—"

"Of course. Of course. What can I do for you?" His smile had changed to a grimace that was twisted into the shape of a smile, but his eyes were definitely missing the warmth.

"Since I'm still employed here, and since my father still has a stake in the business, I came to talk to you about the article that was on the front page of the *Dallas Journal of Business and Development*. Did you read it?"

There was no mistaking how his eyes darkened several shades. "All I can say is that I hope they have a good attorney. Because they're going to get their asses sued. After the dust settles, maybe they'll rename the paper the *Texas Star Journal*."

He laughed at his own joke.

Caroline didn't crack a smile. "Richard, I'm concerned because the story implicates Coopersmith & Bales."

Once again, he donned the cold smile. "Listen, don't worry about it. You just concentrate on your television show and we'll handle everything here."

He stood, but Caroline wasn't leaving until she got the answers she'd been looking for.

"I have it on good authority that the SEC has opened an investigation." She didn't really, but it was a logical next step, if, in fact, everything Drew had told her was true.

"Richard, you are not going to be able to put them off the same way you're trying to put me off. I want some answers, and I want them now. With my father out of the country, it's my duty to protect my family's interest."

Bales laughed, a humorless bark of a laugh. "Your duty? Since when did you decide to take an interest in what was happening here? You're involved in so many other projects that I find it hard to believe you even care. I'll make this very simple for you. All you need to know is that I am not stupid enough to allow myself to go to jail for someone else's greed."

"What is that supposed to mean? You'll let my father take the fall?"

He sighed, a clear message that he was running low on patience. "Your father doesn't have a clue what's going on with the Texas Star account. He's a limited liability partner. So don't worry your pretty little head about him, okay?"

With that condescending remark, he shredded the last of her patience. "Would you lay off the chauvinist remarks? Is this what it would've been like working with you as a senior partner?"

He shook his head. "Right. You as a senior partner. That would've been the day. Although it might have been convenient to have you filling that post. At least you wouldn't have gotten in my way. Take care of yourself, Caroline. Bake me a cake, will you?"

He picked up the phone and turned his back on her. Their meeting was over.

Over the next few days, Caroline watched the Texas Star scandal unfold. Suddenly, the story that had sprouted in the humble newsroom of Dallas's weekly business paper had been grabbed up by all the national media outlets—both print and television. Bia Anderson was credited with breaking the story. She was heralded as the crackerjack reporter who had steadfastly chipped away until she found a chink in the Texas Star armor and had gone in for the kill.

Conspicuously absent from the fray was Drew Montgomery. Soon after the initial hubbub had quieted, Caroline found herself standing at the *Journal*'s modest, dingy white reception desk, asking if she could please have a moment with Drew Montgomery.

"Do you have an appointment?" asked the young woman tending the phones.

"No, I'm sorry, I don't. I was in the neighborhood and I thought I'd stop in."

"Who did you say you were with?"

The irony hit her. She was with no one. As

of right now, the production company hadn't yet come back with a full offer and she was still on hiatus from the firm. She truly wasn't with any-one right now.

"I didn't. Would you please tell him Caroline Coopersmith is here to see him? I just want to say hello."

As the receptionist delivered the message to Drew, it dawned on her that he might very well decline—maybe he would be too busy or she'd relay that he'd just run out on an appointment—even though she'd seen his car in the parking lot.

"He'll be with you in just a moment. You can have a seat over there if you'd like." The woman pointed to the stained white vinyl love seat di-rectly across from the desk.

Her behind had barely hit the vinyl when Drew appeared in the hallway that led to the newsroom. She saw him before he saw her. That's when she glimpsed the look of…what? Hope? Happiness? Disbelief?

She didn't get a chance to discern, because as soon as he saw her, the look slipped from his face and a mask of neutrality replaced it.

"Caroline," he said. "Come on back. Thank you, Donna."

She couldn't read how he felt. He'd thanked

the receptionist with the same level of warmth as
he'd greeted her. Then he walked slightly in front
of her as they headed back to the newsroom. She
imagined that that was how he might treat any
platonic visitor to the office.

The newsroom was abuzz with activity, but
from the bits and pieces she could grab, it sounded
like new business. No residue or remnant of the
Texas Star story, which surprised her. Not that she
expected to find a shrine or trophies or an endless video loop forever commemorating the inci-
dent that on the night she sat in his office—the
last time she saw him or talked to him—seemed
so incredibly insurmountable.

She followed him into his office, and he shut
the door before he unceremoniously took a seat
behind his desk.

He had no hug for her. Not even a kiss on the
cheek. Was that what she had expected?

Well, maybe she had hoped for something a little warmer. Something to indicate that there still
might be a glimmer of hope for them.

"How have you been?" he asked. His voice
cracked and he cleared his throat.

"Busy," she said.

Liar. Okay, she'd had way too much free time

on her hands to worry and wonder and realize just how much she missed him.

"Good," he said. "Me, too."

"I suppose things have been pretty lively since the Texas Star story broke."

There. She said it. Might as well eliminate the elephant in the room from the get-go.

He shrugged. "Not so much. Maybe on the Friday we released the story. That wasn't my story, if you'll remember. So it didn't really affect me that much."

Ouch. Okay.

The silence lasted a couple of beats too long. He wasn't going to make this easy on her, was he? She glanced around his office, taking in the untidy stacks of files and papers that hinted at a man too busy with his passion—work—to worry about incidentals like tidying up.

"Drew, I just came to say that I understand why you had to do what you did with the Texas Star story."

He nodded, but he didn't say anything for a moment.

Finally, he asked, "How's your family?"

"My parents are fine. They just got back from a cruise yesterday. They left shortly after my dad's party."

That night. That fateful night.

"Did he suffer any fallout from the story?"

"Apparently not. I know the SEC has just begun its investigation, but he's a limited liability partner, so culpability would be negligible, if any."

"Uh-huh." His words were monotone. Drew was maintaining his poker face. "Then your family is fine. How are things with Pepper? Fine, too?"

She nodded.

"So, let me ask you a question, Caroline. Are you here today telling me that you understand why I didn't kill the article? Is it all okay because your family escaped the scandal unscathed?"

Oh. So he was still angry with her. Or maybe he just really, truly didn't care about her. The thought made her stomach plummet. Suddenly, coming here seemed like a very bad idea.

"I won't keep you." She stood. In the same place she had the last time she was here. Only this time, she didn't feel nearly as sure of herself as she had then. That's when she saw that the bottle of champagne that she'd brought that night was sitting on the credenza behind his desk.

Wow, she'd really blown it, hadn't she? She'd come to him that night ready to celebrate with him and it ended up being the end of them.

Them. She missed *them* so much she almost couldn't bear it.

"Well, you take care of yourself, okay?" She didn't wait for him to open the door for her or walk her out to the lobby. She made a beeline to her car, got in and drove away as fast as she could.

After he let Caroline walk out of his life for the second time, Drew spent a good portion of the afternoon beating himself up. Why had he acted like such a self-righteous ass?

She'd come there to reach out to him, and he'd all but lectured her on the principles of journalism.

In a moment of protective weakness, she'd asked him to pull a story that she feared might affect her family adversely. She was human.

He was an ass.

He mentally flogged himself until he couldn't stand it anymore. Then he got into his car and drove until he found Caroline. Her car was at the Celebrations, Inc. office. He parked outside and sent her a text. *Look outside*.

A moment later, he saw her open the back door and walk down the driveway. He got out of his car and met her halfway.

"I'm sorry," he said. "I know you're not a journalist, and you might not understand the rules that we play by in that world. I mean, why should you? I couldn't tell you the rules of the accounting world."

She was standing there looking up at him with those emerald eyes, and damn, how he'd missed those lips. He wanted to taste them right now. But first he needed to tell her something.

"At the risk of sounding like a total ass hat, when you asked me to kill the story, it went against every moral fiber in my body. Journalists are the watchdogs of society. If we are going to make this work—this thing that's you and me— you have to understand that I don't get to pick my stories. I have to report the news as it presents itself to me. I can't promise you that anything can be off the record. But I can swear on love itself that I will always be fair."

She was standing there, looking up at him and nodding. So beautiful, it was all he could do to keep from reaching out and pulling her into his arms.

"Is that all?" she asked, a large smile spreading across her face.

"No," he answered. "I've missed you so badly I haven't known which end is up. I love you, Caroline, and I don't want to spend another minute apart."

"I love you, too," she said.

Finally, he gave in to the temptation to touch her, and he pulled her into his arms, enfolding her and holding her tight enough so that they could never lose each other again.

He covered her mouth with his and kissed her soundly and deeply, and she kissed him back like her very life breath depended on him. They didn't stop until the clapping and catcalls brought them back down to earth.

Pepper, Sydney, A.J., Carlos and Lindsay were all standing there cheering them on.

When their cheers finally quieted, Caroline turned to him and asked, "Would you like to be the first to hear about a story that has national news appeal?"

He glanced from Caroline to the exuberant faces of their friends. "You got the show?"

"We got the show! They offered us a contract to shoot the first season of *Celebrations, Inc.* I just found out. Do you want to make some cameo appearances as my man?"

He shook his head. "Nope. No cameos. For that role, it has to be the lead or nothing."

"Are you giving me an ultimatum?" she joked.

"I hope so. Because that's the one area of our lives where I wouldn't have it any other way."

* * * * *

REQUEST YOUR FREE BOOKS!

2 FREE NOVELS PLUS 2 FREE GIFTS!

◆ Harlequin®

SPECIAL EDITION

Life, Love & Family

YES! Please send me 2 FREE Harlequin® Special Edition novels and my 2 FREE gifts (gifts are worth about $10). After receiving them, if I don't wish to receive any more books, I can return the shipping statement marked "cancel." If I don't cancel, I will receive 6 brand-new novels every month and be billed just $4.49 per book in the U.S. or $5.24 per book in Canada. That's a saving of at least 14% off the cover price! It's quite a bargain! Shipping and handling is just 50¢ per book in the U.S. and 75¢ per book in Canada.* I understand that accepting the 2 free books and gifts places me under no obligation to buy anything. I can always return a shipment and cancel at any time. Even if I never buy another book, the two free books and gifts are mine to keep forever.

235/335 HDN FEGF

Name _____ (PLEASE PRINT)

Address _____ Apt. #

City _____ State/Prov. _____ Zip/Postal Code

Signature (if under 18, a parent or guardian must sign)

Mail to the **Reader Service:**
IN U.S.A.: P.O. Box 1867, Buffalo, NY 14240-1867
IN CANADA: P.O. Box 609, Fort Erie, Ontario L2A 5X3

Not valid for current subscribers to Harlequin Special Edition books.

Want to try two free books from another line?
Call 1-800-873-8635 or visit www.ReaderService.com.

* Terms and prices subject to change without notice. Prices do not include applicable taxes. Sales tax applicable in N.Y. Canadian residents will be charged applicable taxes. Offer not valid in Quebec. This offer is limited to one order per household. All orders subject to credit approval. Credit or debit balances in a customer's account(s) may be offset by any other outstanding balance owed by or to the customer. Please allow 4 to 6 weeks for delivery. Offer available while quantities last.

Your Privacy—The Reader Service is committed to protecting your privacy. Our Privacy Policy is available online at www.ReaderService.com or upon request from the Reader Service.

We make a portion of our mailing list available to reputable third parties that offer products we believe may interest you. If you prefer that we not exchange your name with third parties, or if you wish to clarify or modify your communication preferences, please visit us at www.ReaderService.com/consumerschoice or write to us at Reader Service Preference Service, P.O. Box 9062, Buffalo, NY 14269. Include your complete name and address.

HARLEQUIN®

American ★ *Romance*®

Discover the magic of Christmas with two
holiday stories of love and forgiveness in

CHRISTMAS IN TEXAS

Christmas Baby Blessings

by TINA LEONARD

Capri Snow isn't happy when she discovers
that the Bridesmaids Creek Christmastown Santa is her
almost-ex-husband and cop, Seagal West. But when danger
strikes, Seagal steps in to protect his wife, no matter the cost.

&

The Christmas Rescue

by REBECCA WINTERS

When Texas Ranger Flynn Patterson saves Andrea Sinclair
and her infant child from her stalker ex-husband, he finds
himself in more danger than just losing his heart.

**Bring the magic of Christmas home
this November 2012.**

Available wherever books are sold.

When Forever, Texas's newest deputy, Gabe Rodriguez, rescues a woman from the scene of an accident, he encounters a mystery, as well.

Here's a sneak peek at A FOREVER CHRISTMAS by USA TODAY bestselling author Marie Ferrarella, available November 2012 from Harlequin® American Romance®.

It was still raining. Not nearly as bad as it had been earlier but enough to put out what there still was of the fire. Mick was busy hooking up his tow truck to what was left of the woman's charred sedan and Alma was getting back into her Jeep. Neither one of them saw the woman in Gabe's truck suddenly sit up as he started the vehicle.

"No!"

The single word tore from her lips. There was terror in her eyes, and she gave every indication that she was going to jump out of the truck's cab—or at least try to. Surprised, Gabe quickly grabbed her by the arm with his free hand.

"I wouldn't recommend that," he told her.

The fear in her eyes remained. If anything, it grew even greater.

"Who are you?" the blonde cried breathlessly. She appeared completely disoriented.

"Gabriel Rodriguez. I'm the guy who pulled you out of your car and kept you from becoming a piece of charcoal."

Her expression didn't change. It was as if his words weren't even registering. Nonetheless, Gabe paused, giving her a minute as he waited for her response.

But the woman said nothing.

"Okay," he coaxed as he drove toward the town of Forever, "your turn."

The world, both inside the moving vehicle and outside of it, was spinning faster and faster, making it impossible for her to focus on anything. Moreover, she couldn't seem to pull her thoughts together. Couldn't get past the heavy hand of fear that was all but smothering her.

"My turn?" she echoed. What did that mean, her turn? Her turn to do what?

"Yes, your turn," he repeated. "I told you my name. Now you tell me yours."

Her name.

The two words echoed in her brain, encountering only emptiness. Suddenly very weary, she strained hard, searching, waiting for something to come to her.

But nothing did.

The silence stretched out. Finally, just before he repeated his question again, she said in a small voice, hardly above a whisper, "I can't."

Who is this mystery woman?
Find out in A FOREVER CHRISTMAS
by Marie Ferrarella, coming November 2012
from Harlequin® American Romance®.

celebrating 15 YEARS

Love Inspired

CELEBRATE THE HOLIDAYS IN SNOWGLOBE, MONTANA, WITH THESE TWO BRAND-NEW STORIES OF FAITH AND LOVE

Yuletide Homecoming by Linda Goodnight

Five years ago, Rafe Westfield broke his fiancée's heart when he left to join the military. Now the battle-scarred soldier is back in Snowglobe and Amy Caldwell is trying to keep her distance. But holiday events keep bringing Amy and Rafe together... maybe this time forever.

A Family's Christmas Wish by Lissa Manley

Abandoned by her husband when she was eight months pregnant, single mother Sara Kincaid vowed to rely only on herself. But then she makes a deal with handsome widowed father and carpenter Owen Larsen. Can two pint-size matchmakers help them see beyond the past in time for Christmas?

A Snowglobe Christmas

Available November 2012!

HARLEQUIN *Blaze*™
red-hot reads

Double your reading pleasure with Harlequin® Blaze™!

2 GREAT NOVELS SAME GREAT PRICE

As a special treat to you, all Harlequin Blaze books in November will include a new story, plus a classic story by the same author including…

Kate Hoffmann

When Ronan Quinn arrives in Sibleyville, Maine, all he's looking for is a decent job. What he finds instead is a centuries-old curse connected to his family and hostility from all the townsfolk. Only sexy oysterwoman Charlotte Sibley is willing to hire Ronan…and she's about to turn his life upside down.

The Mighty Quinns: Ronan

Look for this new installment of The Mighty Quinns, plus *The Mighty Quinns: Marcus,* the first ever Mighty Quinns book in the same volume!

Available this November wherever books are sold!

www.Harlequin.com